"I . . . I'll trust you,"

Adeline said tentatively, more unnerved by his touch than by what she was promising to do.

"Great." Mac grinned down at her. His beautiful blue eyes seemed to come alive when he smiled. "First things first. We've got to find you somewhere to stay. I know just the place."

"The park bench?" Addy asked cautiously, causing Mac to chuckle.

"No. What I've got in mind is a bit more comfortable. Come on, let's get your bags and I'll show you."

Curious, yet realizing she didn't have much choice in the matter, Addy allowed Mac to collect her lone piece of luggage and lead her out to the parking lot.

She hesitated a moment when they reached his car. "Mac?"

He glanced at her. "What?"

"W-where are we going?"

His eyebrows wiggled in mischief and a smile slanted his lips. "I'm taking you home, of course."

Dear Reader:

Happy holidays! Our authors join me in wishing you all the best for a joyful, loving holiday season with your family and friends. And while celebrating the new year—and the new decade!—I hope you'll think of Silhouette Books.

1990 promises to be especially happy here. This year marks our tenth anniversary, and we're planning a celebration! To symbolize the timelessness of love, as well as the modern gift of the tenth anniversary, each month in 1990, we're presenting readers with a *Diamond Jubilee* Silhouette Romance title, penned by one of your all-time favorite Silhouette Romance authors.

In January, under the Silhouette Romance line's *Diamond Jubilee* emblem, look for Diana Palmer's next book in her bestselling LONG, TALL TEXANS series—*Ethan*. He's a hero sure to lasso your heart! And just in time for Valentine's Day, Brittany Young has written *The Ambassador's Daughter*. Spend the most romantic month of the year in France, the setting for this magical classic. Victoria Glenn, Annette Broadrick, Peggy Webb, Dixie Browning, Phyllis Halldorson—to name just a few!—have written *Diamond Jubilee* titles especially for you. And Pepper Adams has penned a trilogy about three very rugged heroes—and their lovely heroines!—set on the plains of Oklahoma. Look for the first book this summer.

The *Diamond Jubilee* celebration is Silhouette Romance's way of saying thanks to you, our readers. We've been together for ten years now, and with the support you've given us, you can look forward to many more years of heartwarming, poignant love stories.

I hope you'll enjoy this book and all of the stories to come. Come home to romance—Silhouette Romance—for always!

Sincerely,

Tara Hughes Gavin
Senior Editor

SHARON DE VITA

Sweet
Adeline

Silhouette Romance

Published by Silhouette Books New York

America's Publisher of Contemporary Romance

SILHOUETTE BOOKS
300 E. 42nd St., New York, N.Y. 10017

ISBN: 0-373-08693-8

First Silhouette Books printing December 1989

SHARON DE VITA

decided around her thirtieth birthday that she wanted to produce something that didn't have to be walked or fed during the night. An eternal optimist who always believes in happy endings, she felt romances were the perfect vehicle for her creative energies. As a reader and a writer, she prefers stories that are fun and light-hearted and tries to inject these qualities into her own work. The mother of three, she has been happily married to her high school sweetheart for eighteen years.

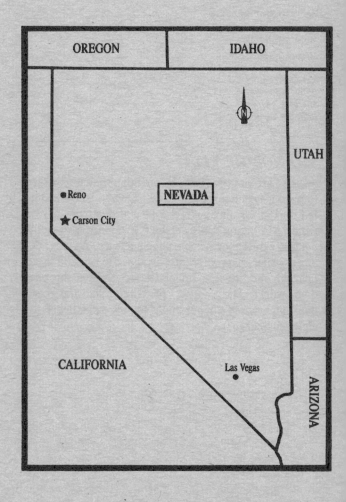

Chapter One

After ten years in Vegas, MacArthur "Mac" Cole knew trouble when he saw it. The moment he laid eyes on the woman standing in his office with her lips pursed like an angry archangel on judgment day, he *knew* she was going to be trouble. She looked as out of place in a glittering casino as a cootie at a cockfight.

What was she doing up here? he wondered in annoyance. And how the hell had she gotten past security? His office was off-limits to everyone, particularly—no—*especially* to casino guests.

Preparing himself for yet another problem, Mac heaved a weary sigh then planted himself firmly in the open doorway. "Can I help you?"

The deep booming masculine voice caused Adeline Simpson to whirl. Her jaw dropped and she gasped, taking an involuntary step backward as her gaze collided with the man filling the doorway. Merciful Heaven, it was Lucifer himself, she thought with absolute certainty.

"What are you doing in my office?" Mac demanded with a frown, wondering what her problem was. Her jaw had flapped open as if it had come unhinged.

"I'm...I'm...ah..." Swallowing the ball of cotton wedged in the back of her throat, Adeline tried to find her tongue. The man's sheer size, not to mention his unconventional appearance had thrown her momentarily off guard. She felt as if the ground beneath her had given way. "I'm...I'm..." Straightening her frame, Adeline squared her delicate shoulders and met the man's steely gaze. "I'm looking for MacArthur Cole."

"Well, you've found him." Mac crossed the room toward his desk. "But the name's Mac," he growled, causing her to tense.

"You're MacArthur Cole?" Adeline's eyes sprung open and her heart beat a wicked dance beneath her starched high-collared blouse as she stared at the massive man in wide-eyed terror. Merciful Heaven, he was as big as the truck he was named for! Pitch-black hair was brushed casually off a high forehead. His chin was square and his cheekbones were high and blunt. His lips were full and tugged downward in obvious displeasure. There was a silent moment of shock before Adeline noticed the long jagged scar that ran from one ear, down his cheek, almost to his Adam's apple. Nature had carved his features with bold strokes, giving him an intense, weather-beaten look. He was the most masculine man Adeline had ever met. And he scared her to death.

Clutching her small handbag closer to her trembling chest, Adeline struggled to find her composure. Under normal circumstances a man who looked like him would have sent her scurrying for the nearest police officer. But these weren't normal circumstances, Adeline sternly chided herself.

"Now that we know who *I* am," Mac said pointedly, uncoiling his long lean frame into the chair behind his desk, "why don't you tell me who the hell you are?"

Adeline blanched. "There's certainly no reason to use profanity, Mr. Cole," she scolded, causing Mac to glance up at her in surprise. "My name is Adeline Simpson," she informed him, lowering herself to a chair opposite him. "And I need your help."

Mac rubbed the side of his face and sighed heavily. Just what he needed today—another disgruntled tourist who had gambled more than she should have. She probably needed bus fare to get home.

"How much did you lose?" he growled, preparing to give her his standard lecture about gambling with money you couldn't afford to lose.

"I'm afraid you don't understand—"

"I understand perfectly," Mac assured her, ignoring the frown that creased her brow.

"No, you don't," Adeline insisted, wondering why the man was staring at her so intently. It only increased her anxiety. "I haven't lost.. .." She faltered a bit, totally unnerved by the man. "Well, it's not money that I've lost." She took a deep breath to gather her courage and plunged on. "You see, Mr. Cole, I have reason to believe my grandfather is here, in this casino, and I want *you* to help me find him."

"You want *me* to what?" Mac bellowed, startling Adeline so much she nearly came clean out of the chair.

"There's no need to shout," Adeline reprimanded him, twisting her damp hands nervously in her lap. "I said *I'd like you to help me find my grandfather.*"

Mac looked at her incredulously. She was sitting ramrod straight, with her legs primly crossed and her skirt pulled low to cover her knees. Her blouse was white and frayed a bit around the edges; it was buttoned so high up on her neck he wondered how she swallowed. Her skirt was a mud brown and covered more leg than he'd seen covered in a month of Sundays. In a town where women dressed to reveal more than they concealed, he couldn't help but wonder what *this* woman was hiding beneath all that cloth.

She wasn't beautiful, he decided, but she was damned attractive. Her hair was the color of fresh wheat, parted down the middle and pulled back into a braid that hung down her back. Her skin was as clear and smooth as alabaster, complementing huge green eyes fringed by inky black lashes. For some reason she reminded him of Alice in Wonderland. He fought down a smile. Beautiful green eyes or not, he had much too much to do today to get suckered into helping her.

"This is a casino, lady," Mac growled, causing her spirits to droop along with the corners of her mouth. "*Not* the lost and found." He shook his head, sighing heavily again. Obviously this woman's channel wasn't tuned to the right station. Why him? he wondered in disgust. It wasn't enough that some con man had managed to elude the casino's sophisticated security system and was now working a scam that was costing the casino a bundle on a daily basis. Now he had some wide-eyed innocent thinking he was the missing persons bureau! Even his patience had limits, and he certainly didn't need this—or her—today.

"Why do I have to get all the kooks?" Mac wondered aloud, causing Adeline to scowl at him.

"Sir," she defended hotly, "I am not a kook!"

Mac leveled a gaze at her that should have sent her scurrying toward the nearest exit. "Miss Simpson," he began slowly, enunciating each and every word as if he were talking to a slightly daft child. "I want you to listen to me *very* carefully. I'm going to close my eyes and count to ten, and when I open my eyes, I expect that chair to be empty and *you* to be gone. Got it?" His eyes narrowed and darkened, causing her to tremble.

"But—"

"Got it?" Mac repeated. His tone of voice was not meant to soothe. It didn't.

Taking a deep breath, Adeline realized she was trembling. Stop this, Adeline, she chided herself, allowing her temper to flare. She hadn't traveled nearly three thousand miles only to turn tail and bolt at the first sign of trouble. Even if that trouble was in the form of a mountain of a man who had the ability to scare her witless just by the tone of his voice.

Where was her sturdy midwestern pride? Her backbone? Back home in Muncie, Indiana, safe and sound, she decided grimly.

Gathering up her dwindling courage, Adeline dug deep for some of that pride. MacArthur Cole could issue all the orders he liked, she decided stubbornly, but she wasn't budging from this town or this office until she found Grandpa. And this rude mountain of a man sitting with his head back and his eyes closed in an effort to ignore her was going to help her whether he liked it or not. And whether he knew it or not. Well, one could only hope, she thought lamely.

Determined to wait him out, Adeline sighed, then ran one finger around the sticky high-necked collar of her blouse before carefully smoothing back an errant strand of hair that had come loose from her braid. She had not been prepared for the intense heat of Nevada. Back home in Muncie, spring would just be blooming, but here in Las Vegas, the sun blazed as hot as a blustering inferno. Adeline gently patted her upper lip. Merciful Heaven, it was worse than a steam bath.

Mac slowly opened one eye, not in the least bit surprised to still find her there. "You're still here," he announced unnecessarily. From the determined look on her face, he had a feeling she wasn't about to leave until he heard her out or threw her out. Though the latter sounded more appealing than the former, Mac knew he couldn't do it. He'd always been a sucker for a hard-luck story, particularly when it was accompanied by enormous green eyes.

"All right," he said in disgust, more irritated at himself than with her. "I'll give you exactly five minutes." He glanced at the thin gold watch on his wrist. "Start talking."

Annoyed by his rudeness, Adeline bit her tongue to keep from telling him what she thought of his manners. "Yes, well, Grandpa disappeared two days ago, and I've been out of my mind with worry. He's never done anything like that. I mean it was so unlike him." Mac heaved an irritating sigh and Adeline rushed on. "Anyway, yesterday, Aunt Myrtle let it slip out. I know she didn't mean to, I could tell by the way she flushed and—"

"Three minutes," Mac reminded her, glancing at his watch again. Adeline's temper erupted.

"Are you always so rude?" she demanded, eyes blazing. "Back home in Muncie, guests are treated with regard and respect, not like some…intruding vermin." Her chin lifted haughtily. "Why I've seen stray mutts receive better receptions!"

Stunned by her heated outburst, Mac leaned back in his chair and regarded her intently. It had been a long time since anyone had had the audacity, never mind the guts, to speak to him in such a manner. He was a rich, powerful man; respect automatically came with the territory. Obviously this woman didn't give two bits about his position, never mind his financial status. Mac had to admit her behavior was a refreshing change from the usual yes-men that surrounded him. Interesting, he thought, as a shadow of a smile played along his lips. Very interesting.

There was obviously much more to this prim little woman than met the eye. She sure had guts, he thought in sudden

admiration. He wondered if she knew how her eyes sparkled and how her mouth pouted with temper when she was
angry. Mac suddenly wondered how her mouth would look
when properly kissed. A wave of desire rolled over him,
startling him. It had been a long, long time since a woman
had captured his curiosity. And Mac suddenly found himself inordinately curious about the feisty Miss Simpson from
Muncie, Indiana.

"Two minutes, Miss Simpson," Mac warned, suddenly
anxious to get her out of his office and out of his vision. He
didn't know if he was more annoyed by her and her outlandish story, whatever it was, or by his unusual reaction to
her. Opening his desk drawer, Mac dragged out a crumpled
pack of cigarettes, pulled one loose, lit it, and then regarded her through a haze of smoke before remembering he
had quit smoking a week ago. Muttering an oath of disgust, he crushed the cigarette out into a nearby ashtray, silently cursing Miss Simpson for distracting him.

Realizing the man's patience was nearing the limit, Adeline rushed on with her story. "You see, Grandpa and I have
seven hundred and forty-three dollars—"

"Congratulations," Mac said, causing her to scowl at
him. She opened her mouth to reply, then snapped it shut,
changing her mind.

"Anyway, the taxes on Simpson House have unexpect-
edly tripled this year. In exactly one week we will owe the
assessor two thousand, two hundred and twenty-nine dollars." Adeline paused to take a deep breath, vividly aware
that this man was looking at her as if he expected someone
with a net to descend on her at any moment and haul her
off. "Anyway, Grandpa and I don't have the extra money
we need to pay the—"

"Wait a minute." Mac held up his hand to stop her lit-
any. "What the hell is Simpson House?"

"It's the family home. It's been in my father's family for generations. After my mother passed away, Grandpa and Aunt Myrtle came back to Muncie to raise me. They turned Simpson House into a small retirement home in order to support us." Adeline leaned forward in her chair. Her huge green eyes were filled with a silent plea. "But now the taxes are due and we don't have the funds to pay them. We can't lose Simpson House, we simply can't. If we lose Simpson House, where will we go?"

Mac stared at her calmly, trying to decide if she was dangerous or not.

"Then, of course," Adeline went on, looking thoroughly distressed, "there's Walter. Aunt Myrtle couldn't bear to give him up. Why, he's been with her forever."

One dark eyebrow rose as Mac tried to make sense out of her ramblings. Obviously she was going to get to the point, but he had a feeling they both might be ready for Medicare before she did. "Who's Walter?" he asked, trying to keep up with her.

"Aunt Myrtle's pigeon," she replied calmly, as if there weren't anything unusual about it. "I'm sure you know there aren't many places that allow pets, and it would just break her heart— What's so funny, Mr. Cole?" she asked coldly as a smile twitched at the corners of his mouth.

Mac leaned back and absently rubbed his chin. His eyes danced in amusement. "Are you...ah...trying to tell me you have a *pigeon named Walter*?"

She nodded her head and Mac tried not to grin. Obviously this woman's seven hundred dollars would be better spent on some good psychiatric help. *"Walter Pigeon,"* he said, chuckling to himself.

"I hardly see what's so funny, Mr. Cole," Adeline snapped indignantly. "Walter is very much a part of our little family. Aunt Myrtle's quite attached to him. Why, it would break her heart if she had to give him up."

"Oh, I'm sure," Mac murmured, nodding his head as if he believed every word she said. He couldn't quite decide if he should press the hidden button under his desk that would fill his office with security guards or let her go on. He decided to let her continue; he couldn't wait to hear the rest of this story.

"If we lose Simpson House, where will we go?" Adeline asked, looking at Mac as if he had the answer. He shrugged his shoulders helplessly. Not only did he not know the answer, he wasn't quite sure he knew the question. "Grandpa and Aunt Myrtle are retired and living on a small pension. They can't move just anywhere; financially it's simply impossible." Her eyes darkened with pride. "Grandpa and I promised that we would spend the rest of our days together, and I have never broken a promise, Mr. Cole, and I'm certainly not about to start now."

Despite his misgivings, Mac found himself entranced by this rather peculiar woman and her outlandish story.

"I still don't see what all this has to do with me," Mac said. Forgetting himself, he lit another cigarette.

"That's where Grandpa comes in. I'm afraid he's about to do something foolish." Adeline's glance met Mac's and she quickly looked away. He had the most arresting eyes. They were the palest shade of blue, like a wolf's, she thought absently, and quite unlike any she had ever seen. They gave her the feeling the man could see through her, reading her deepest, darkest, most private thoughts. It was totally disconcerting.

"Go on, Miss Simpson," Mac prodded, wondering why she refused to meet his gaze. Every time she did, a slight rosy hue dotted her cheeks. It was really quite becoming.

"Yes...well..." Adeline fidgeted with her handbag, deliberately avoiding Mac's gaze. She was normally not the kind of person to open up and unburden herself and her problems. Why, there were some things she hadn't ever told

Pernall Ditkus, and she'd been keeping company with him since they were children. But under the circumstances she really had no choice.

Adeline's lips compressed in vexation. There were just some things a lady shouldn't have to do, she thought sourly. One was to beg for help from impudent strangers, and the other was to renege on one's obligations. To her extreme displeasure, Adeline now found herself in imminent danger of doing both. But it couldn't be helped, she assured herself stoically, and there was no point in lollygagging around, lamenting her misfortune. She was much too practical to waste time feeling sorry for herself. She had to find her grandfather—and soon—before he did something foolish. And this man, this rude, irritating MacArthur Cole was going to help her whether he wanted to or not.

She could be just as stubborn as the next person when the need arose, Adeline decided, forcing herself to meet Mac's curious stare and go on.

"Anyway, after Grandpa disappeared, I was frantic. Yesterday Aunt Myrtle let it slip that I might find him here, in this casino. I also discovered that Grandpa had withdrawn all but one hundred dollars from our account. That was the money we had saved for the property taxes, and I'm afraid he's come to Las Vegas, to this casino," she added pointedly, "to do something foolish."

"Something foolish?" Mac repeated, and Adeline sighed.

"Yes, I'm afraid that Grandpa plans to try his hand at gambling in order to win the money we need to pay the taxes."

"So?" Mac brought his befuddled gaze to hers.

"So!" Adeline fumed, wondering why on earth she had ever expected a man like him to understand. After all, he *was* a gambler. An invisible shudder shook her frame. Thank goodness her late mother would never know that the future of the Simpson family home rested on the shoulders of someone as lascivious as a gambler.

Her mother had passed along the sturdy, midwestern values that Adeline lived her life by: respect for law and order, honoring one's obligations and a hard day's work for a hard day's pay. Naturally this man wouldn't be able to understand that gambling was certainly not something she could condone—no matter what the circumstances.

"Mr. Cole," she said frostily. "I don't approve of gambling."

"Neither do I," Mac shot back. "Just because I own this casino doesn't mean I'm a gambler. I could never remain in this town, or in this business, if I was. I'm a businessman," Mac said casually, leaning back in his chair. "The business I'm in is one of supply and demand. I supply what the customer wants, and in this case it happens to be gambling." He smiled and Adeline averted her gaze to a spot directly over his right shoulder.

Perhaps it would be easier to think if she didn't have to look directly into his beautiful blue eyes. It caused an uncommon warmth to uncurl in the depths of her belly. MacArthur Cole was, as Great-Grandmother Simpson used to say, "a fine figure of a man," and he made her incredibly nervous.

"Adeline," Mac began slowly. "It seems to me you're between a rock and a hard place. You don't have the money to pay the taxes anyway. So if your grandfather wants to try his hand at gambling to make the rest of the money, what's the harm? You've got nothing to lose."

"No," she said firmly, shaking her head and causing her braid to swing to and fro. "My grandfather is a quiet, respectable man. He has no experience with this type of activity. He's never gambled in his life. Why, he won't even participate in bingo at the church socials. If he attempts this foolishness, I'm sure he's going to lose. Then what? No, I simply can't allow it. That's why I have to find him—soon. Besides, circumstances have changed in the last twenty-four hours and..." Her voice trailed off and she lifted her gaze to his. Mac saw a faint shadow of worry cloud her eyes and wondered what had caused it.

She was getting to him, he decided in disgust. This little slip of a woman with her prim clothes and huge green eyes was actually getting to him. He was beginning to believe her outlandish story!

She lifted her chin. "By the end of the week, I could have the additional money we need to pay the taxes."

"How'd you get the money?" he asked, startling Adeline by his directness. Mac cocked his head and looked at her shrewdly. Something wasn't right; he could feel it in his bones. He now found himself more intrigued than annoyed.

Adeline felt a hot rush of warmth rise from beneath the collar of her blouse to cover her face. She wished she had learned to lie or at least shade the truth. It would come in handy particularly in situations like this, but alas, she'd never learned. Every time she even shaded the truth, a red splotchy rash broke out all about her neck.

"Pernall Ditkus has proposed marriage," she said quietly, embarrassed and not knowing why.

Mac's dark brows drew together in a decided frown. "What the hell is a Pernall Ditkus?" Sounded like some rare strain of virus.

"He's...that is..." Adeline swallowed nervously. How could she explain to this...stranger who Pernall was? She couldn't even put a name on their relationship. They had known each other since they were children. They had been friends—buddies—really. Their relationship had never been one of a romantic nature, despite Adeline's mother's best efforts to make it so. More than anything else, Adeline's mother had wanted her to marry Pernall. In fact, it had been her dying request, along with saving Simpson House. But Adeline had evaded Pernall for all these years.

In the past year, though, Pernall's mother had been ailing, and he had been putting pressure on Adeline to marry him. She had a feeling Pernall's proposal had more to do with his fear of being alone rather than any great love interest. She had always politely refused him, until the problem with the taxes arose. Pernall had offered to pay the taxes on Simpson House if she would agree to marry him. It was more like a business transaction than a romantic commitment. She would get the money she needed to save Simpson House, and Pernall would get the companionship he needed, plus someone to look after his ailing mother in her final days. Adeline had promised Pernall she would think about his proposal and give him her answer in a week.

Thoughts of Pernall brought on a rush of guilt. She hadn't even told him she was leaving Muncie. When he found out she had just up and taken off, he would be livid, particularly when he found out it had been to find her grandfather. Pernall and Grandpa had never been crazy about each other.

If Pernall ever found out *where she was and what she was doing.... Merciful Heaven!* Adeline banished the thought. She couldn't waste time worrying about Pernall's admonishments now. She had to find her grandfather. Somehow she'd find a way to explain, to make Pernall understand. But she'd worry about that later.

Squaring her shoulders, Adeline met Mac's curious gaze. "Pernall is the man I've been keeping company with."

"Keeping company," Mac repeated, his voice a bit shocked. He hadn't heard that expression since women wore high-topped shoes. "So what does this guy's proposal have to do with the extra money you need?" Mac watched her carefully. Adeline nervously twisted her hands and shifted her slender frame. He had a feeling he had struck a nerve.

A sudden thought caused a pain from the past to rise up like bile in his throat. "I get it," Mac said, shaking his head in disgust. "He offered you the money for the taxes if you married him, right?"

"Well, it's not quite as heartless as you make it seem." Her face flamed and Mac knew he was right. Normally he wouldn't stick his nose into other people's business, but this woman had made her business *his* business.

"Seems to me it's you who's about to do something foolish," he said quietly, and Adeline's gaze flew to his.

Her chin went up. "I beg your pardon?" she said coldly, holding his gaze despite the fact that it made her insides quake like a sapling in a storm.

"Have you ever done any gambling, Adeline?" Mac inquired.

"Certainly not." She frowned suddenly, wondering where he was leading. "Of course I do play bingo once a month. But I don't really consider that gambling."

"Bingo," Mac muttered drolly, dragging a hand through his hair. "There're two rules in gambling, Adeline. The first is never gamble with more than you can afford to lose."

"And the second?"

Mac grinned. *"Never forget the first."*

"I really don't see what all of this has to do with me and Pernall."

Mac's features sobered. "Seems to me what you're gambling with this Parsnips fellow—"

"Pernall," she corrected in irritation, pressing her lips together.

Mac waved his hand in the air. "Yeah, whatever. Seems to me you're gambling with more than you can afford to lose. Marrying a man simply because he offers you... how much?" Mac mentally calculated the amount, then shook his head. After all these years in Vegas, there weren't many things left that shocked Mac, but for some reason, this did.

"You're promising to spend your life with someone in exchange for fourteen hundred and some odd bucks!" Mac said, clearly appalled at the situation. "If that ain't a gamble, I don't know what is." He cocked his head and looked at her. His eyes were soft and warm, and Adeline felt something flare deep inside. Her pulse thrummed behind the collar of her blouse.

"Seems to me you're selling yourself short, Adeline," Mac continued, deliberately softening his voice. "An attractive woman like yourself should have a better reason to marry someone than fourteen hundred dollars."

An attractive woman like yourself. Adeline stared at Mac in wonder as his words reverberated through her mind. In all her life, in all twenty-three years, no one had ever told her she was attractive. Merciful Heaven, it made her heart pound like a jackhammer.

MacArthur Cole was an extremely handsome and virile man. The thought that someone like *him* found her attractive... Her lashes slid closed. All her life she had wondered what it would feel like to have a man's attention, to have a man's eyes follow her every movement, to have a man think she was attractive.

Adeline sighed in resignation. She was much too practical to feel sorry for herself or give in to flights of fancy. Long ago she had faced the fact that she was no raving beauty.

Adeline, you'd better develop your mind, for no man will come calling for your looks.

Adeline, it's no sin to be plain. Keep yourself clean and presentable, and then maybe someday...

Her mother's words echoed through Adeline's mind. She had followed her mother's advice. She had developed her mind and kept herself clean and presentable. She was still keeping company with Pernall, but Adeline hadn't yet found the courage to agree to marry him.

To no one would Adeline admit that sometimes at night she lay awake in bed, wondering if perhaps there wasn't more to life than Pernall.

Years ago, when she was very young, she had told her mother all about her dreams to travel and see what else life had to offer besides Muncie.

"You're just like your grandfather," her mother had scolded. "Ungrateful and selfish. Adeline, it's a sin to want more when others have so much less. You have to learn to appreciate what you have."

Adeline had been suffused with guilt for her wanderlust thoughts and feelings. Then her mother died, and Adeline had always wondered if her mother's illness was her penance for yearning for more and not appreciating what she had. Adeline realized that she had been selfish and ungrateful, but then it had been too late. Her mother was gone. It had all been so confusing to her.

So Adeline had buried her dreams and decided to stay in Muncie because she knew it's what her mother would have wanted. She taught herself to appreciate what she had and never yearn for more. It had always been enough. Until now.

Until the prospect of actually marrying Pernall and spending the rest of her life with him loomed on the horizon, growing closer with each passing day.

"Adeline?" Mac's deep voice caused her eyes to fly open. Blinking rapidly, she banished her memories. There was no point in feeling sorry for herself. There was stability and security in knowing what each day would bring even if it was a bit . . . boring at times. But it was more than many others had.

"Can't you borrow the money for taxes? Surely there must be—" Mac stopped as she shook her head ferociously, causing her braid to swing.

"I can't do that," she said quietly. "I've never borrowed money from anyone in my life. Grandpa and I have always managed to take care of our bills and live within our means by paying cash. I owe no quarter to any man. And now..." Her voice faltered a bit. "And now," Adeline continued, swallowing her pride, "it seems as if I have no credit. The banks have refused to give me a loan without any references."

"But what about your family? You must have someone other than your grandfather and what's his name."

"There's no one," she admitted. "Just Grandpa and me, and of course, Aunt Myrtle."

"Of course." Mac nodded his head in understanding. He knew what it was like to have no one and nowhere to turn. All he had was his sister, Rosie, and the casino. But there had been a time in his life when he hadn't even had that. He knew what it was like to have your back against the wall. Mac remembered the feeling and he didn't like it, not at all.

"What about assets?" Mac asked gently, finding that he was being drawn deeper and deeper into this in spite of himself. "You must have something you could sell or use as collateral?"

Adeline nervously fingered the brooch at her neck and shook her head dismally. The brooch had been given to her by her grandfather when she graduated from high school. It was her only piece of jewelry and she could never bear to part with it. It meant more than anything to her, especially since her grandfather had given it to her.

"I've already thought of that," she said quietly, continuing to finger the brooch, "but I have little else other than Simpson House." Her lashes lowered for an instant before she brought her gaze back to his. "I've never really had a need for...things."

Mac suddenly understood the frayed collar and cuffs of her blouse. In a town where anything could be had for a price, Adeline Simpson was like a spring flower in a patch of weeds. It was a rare commodity, at least in his experience, to find someone who wasn't possessed by *things*.

Adeline was proud, stubborn and loyal. He could imagine what it had cost her to come to him and ask for his help. He had to admire her. In some ways, she was just like him. Alone and proud and not wanting to ask for help from anyone. Perhaps that's why she touched a soft spot in him.

"Adeline," Mac said, getting up from his chair and walking around his desk. He perched on one corner and looked at her. She trembled at the expression in his eyes. He had a way of looking at her that made her feel as if she was the only thing in the world. *His world*. "Have you considered selling Simpson House?"

Adeline jerked upright in her chair. "Oh, no," she breathed, her hand flying to her open mouth. "I could never consider selling Simpson House." Adeline had promised her mother before she died that no matter what, she would hang on to Simpson House at any cost. If the cost was her hand in marriage, then . . .

"Selling the place has to be better than marrying some guy because he promises to bail you out of a tight spot." Mac couldn't help but wonder what kind of a guy had to buy a woman's hand in marriage. He remembered another woman who had married as a means for security, and he knew firsthand where it would lead. But did Adeline? He doubted it.

"Pernall's offer was very generous," Adeline said quietly, glancing away. A flush of color dotted her cheeks and Mac instantly regretted his hasty tongue.

"I'm sorry," he said, reaching out to touch her hand. Her delicate skin tingled at his touch and she raised her eyes to his. "I didn't mean to offend you." Mac enfolded her hand in his, suddenly entranced by her. His eyes met hers, and for a long, silent moment time stood still as they stared at each other.

Her heart thudded wickedly against her breast. She could feel her blood rushing through her ears. It was an unfamiliar experience and a quick hot thrill raced through her.

"Will you help me find my grandfather?" she whispered. Mac's gaze still held hers, and for the first time in Adeline's life she was lost in the depths of a man's attention. It felt wonderful. Exhilarating. She dragged her gaze from his to stare at their joined hands. He had nice hands, she thought. Strong hands. Kind hands. *A man's hands.* She could imagine Mac chopping wood with those hands, or soothing a crying child, or caressing a woman. Oh, Lord, where on earth had that thought come from? Perhaps the heat and the jet lag had scrambled her wits. She shouldn't be thinking such things about a man she barely knew. But he was so different from Pernall. So very different.

Pernall was soft and round, not hard and strong like Mac. The comparison between the two of them was so stark it was hard for her to ignore.

Adeline swallowed hard and slowly withdrew her hand from Mac's as guilt washed over her. She shouldn't be holding hands with one man while supposedly thinking over a proposal from another.

When Adeline pulled her hand free, Mac took a deep breath. Something about Adeline touched him in ways he'd never been touched before. For some reason he was unwilling to let this woman just up and walk out of his office and possibly out of his life. He wanted—no needed—to know more about her.

Mac stood up and rounded his desk again. Taking a seat, he grabbed a pen, knowing he would probably hate himself in the morning. He sighed heavily. Damn those wide green eyes, he thought in amusement.

"Tell me all you can about your grandfather," Mac said with a smile, "and I'll see what I can do." What was one more problem? Besides, what would life be like without problems? Dull, he decided, watching Adeline's face light up with a beautiful smile.

She scooted forward in her chair, her eyes shining in excitement. She felt giddy and she didn't know why, but she had a feeling MacArthur Cole had something to do with it.

"Grandpa's about sixty-six," Adeline said with a laugh. "But I can't vouch for that, because his age is a closely guarded secret. He's about five foot seven, with silver hair and deep green eyes. He's quite dapper, and very smooth. He favors three-piece suits, wears a gold pocket watch in his vest and generally smokes those skinny little cigars when he thinks I'm not looking."

Mac took notes, his pen moving rapidly against the page.

"I've checked at the front desk, but they refused to tell me if he was registered or not."

"Company policy," Mac informed her with a smile. "Anything else?"

"Grandpa walks with a cane, the result of an old war wound." Chewing her bottom lip in thought, Adeline searched her mind for additional information. "His name's Robert La Rue, but once in a while one of his friends will call him Blackie. I guess it's an old nickname, although I don't know how on earth he— What's wrong?" she asked abruptly as Mac's pen came to a halt and he threw it down on his desk. His jaw tightened and he looked up at her. He muttered an oath under his breath. He had been right, she *was* going to be trouble. Damn!

"I'm sorry, Adeline," Mac said with sincere regret. "I don't think I can help you."

Adeline frowned in confusion, stunned by the abrupt change in Mac's behavior. "But I thought you just said—"

"Look," he said, getting to his feet. "I told you I can't help you." He forced himself to spit out his next words. "This is a casino. Not the lost and found." He watched her eyes change from anger to defiance and felt a wave of regret. "I'm sorry."

"Sorry!" Adeline exploded, jumping to her feet. Hot salty tears of embarrassment burned her cheeks. To have lowered herself to ask for—no, *beg* for—help, and then been insulted and humiliated was too much for her to handle in her distressed state. "You are the most—the most—" At a loss for words, Adeline snatched her purse up and clutched it to her trembling chest. "Mr. Cole, you are the most ill-mannered human being it has ever been my displeasure to meet. But you're not going to stop me," she cried, desperately fighting back tears. "I'm going to find my grandfather, with or without your help!"

"Adeline, wait," Mac called, wanting to stop her but knowing he couldn't.

"And if you won't help me find him," she yelled over her shoulder, "I'll find *someone* who will!" Adeline spun on her heel and stormed out of Mac's office, slamming the door soundly behind her.

"Damn," Mac muttered, grabbing the telephone receiver and quickly punching out a number. The phone was picked up immediately.

"Blackie," Mac barked. "Why the hell didn't you tell me about your granddaughter?"

Chapter Two

My *granddaughter*?'' came Blackie's startled reply. ''What's Adeline got to do with this?''

''Your granddaughter's *here*,'' Mac informed him. ''In Las Vegas.''

''*Here!* In Las Vegas?'' There was a long, pregnant pause. ''Hell's bells,'' Blackie bellowed. ''What the blazes is Addy doing here?''

''Looking for you,'' Mac replied drolly, wishing he could see the look on the dapper, unflappable Blackie La Rue's face.

At one time Blackie La Rue had been one of the best con men in the gambling business. In their adventurous youth, Blackie and Mac's grandfather, Frankie, had wreaked havoc on casino owners all across Nevada. Just the sight of the two of them was enough to cause casino bosses to shiver in their boots and lock their vaults, and not necessarily in that order.

Blackie La Rue and Frankie Parkland were the very best at relieving unsuspecting casino owners of their money. The casinos called it cheating; Blackie and Frankie called it evening the odds. The duo was perfectly harmless, if a bit sticky fingered. They enjoyed their work and counted among their friends some of the most notorious gamblers in the world. Blackie La Rue and Frankie Parkland were legends in their own time.

Until one day, when Blackie and Mac's grandfather decided to put their considerable talents together and go for one last shot at the pot of gold. They'd made a big score—one that was still talked about with reverence around the strip—and used their ill-gotten gains to open their own casino.

Their casino, named the Parkland, flourished. No one could con a con man. Blackie and Frankie knew all the tricks of the trade. For several years the unbeatable duo reigned supreme in Las Vegas.

But something happened—what—Mac never did learn—and one day Blackie just disappeared. Frankie carried on without him, never once questioning his partner's sudden disappearance. If Frankie knew the reason for Blackie's departure, he never let on. The secret went with him to his grave.

When Frankie passed away, he left the casino and his legacy to his grandson, Mac, and his granddaughter, Rosie.

Mac had carried on as the Parkland's owner, while Rosie had taken over the reins as head of security. Rosie and Mac had learned the casino business from the best—their grandfather.

What they *hadn't* learned was how to stop or identify a con. Their grandfather, who had become a respectable businessman, refused to divulge to his grandchildren the knowledge he'd gained during his adventurous youth. They were vividly aware of what he had done, but not *how he had done it*.

It never really bothered Mac until a few months ago when the Parkland became the victim of a very sophisticated con, the likes of which neither Mac nor Rosie had ever seen. A con that even their sophisticated computerized security system couldn't seem to discover. Mac's first thought was Blackie La Rue. He was certain his grandfather's former partner was back in business again.

Blackie's whereabouts were still unknown after all these years, but Mac put the best private investigators in the country on the case, only to learn that Blackie La Rue was safely ensconced in some place called Muncie, Indiana.

Even though Blackie was ruled out as the culprit, the con continued, with the casino losing more money day by day. Rosie had the best security people on the case, but nothing turned up. They had no idea how the culprit was managing to outwit their sophisticated security system.

In desperation, Mac decided to play a hunch. He called Blackie and quickly explained the situation. He knew the man probably still considered himself the ultimate professional, so he deliberately hinted that although Blackie was probably too old and too out of touch to do anything about the situation, perhaps he could recommend some course of action.

Just as Mac suspected, Blackie was thoroughly and utterly insulted. He blustered a bit about wet-behind-the-ears ingrates, then went on to insist the years had tarnished neither his skills nor his knowledge.

Naturally offended, Blackie offered his services, much to Mac's delight. But Blackie had two stipulations: One, no one was to know Blackie La Rue was back in town or in business. And second, Mac had to let Blackie operate on his own and in his own way. Mac quickly agreed. It was a small price to pay to keep the coffers of the Parkland safe. Once the terms were agreed upon, Mac promised Blackie one-half of everything the con man had gotten if—and it was a big if—Blackie could catch him. The money was worth the gamble to Mac.

"Hell's bells," Blackie cried again. "How the blazes did Addy find me?"

"Seems your sister—"

"Myrtle," Blackie moaned. "I should have known better. That woman . . . I tell you she's been living with that pigeon too long. What does Addy want?"

Mac grinned derisively. "What else? To find you."

"Find me?" Blackie cried, horrified at the implications. For all of his granddaughter's life he had been trying desperately to get her to do something adventurous and daring. He had tried to get Adeline to sample some of the banquets life had to offer, but without much success. Until now.

But, Merciful Heaven, did she have to decide *now* was the time to take his advice? Blackie wondered morosely. Her timing couldn't have been worse. This was the last thing he needed. If she ever found out . . . "Did you tell Addy anything?" he asked suspiciously.

"Not a thing," Mac replied. "I promised not to tell anyone about you or your whereabouts. That was our deal, remember? I'm a man of my word, Blackie."

"Thank goodness," Blackie whispered in obvious relief.

"Blackie, what's going on? What is she doing here?" Mac adjusted his legs in a more comfortable position atop his desk, prepared to hear another one of Blackie's entertaining, if not altogether truthful stories.

"Well, Mac," Blackie began, obviously stalling. "You see, my granddaughter thinks I'm just a nice retired gentleman with a small pension. She doesn't quite know anything about my . . . my . . . illustrious past."

Mac couldn't help it, he started to chuckle. The idea of Blackie as a harmless retiree on a small pension was like saying World War II had been a mild skirmish.

"I want to keep it that way, Mac," Blackie insisted firmly. "There's no reason for the child to learn any differently. She's accepted me all these years for who she thinks I am, and I don't want anything to change that."

Mac frowned. "I don't understand, Blackie, what possible difference could it make? You've been out of business for years."

"Yes, well, I'm not so sure that makes any difference, Mac. You see, my daughter, Florence, that was Addy's mother, she took a dim view of my...occupation. Considered me a disgrace, she did. In fact, she moved to Indiana, married a man steeped in generations of respectability and pretended she'd never heard of me. I wasn't quite good enough for Florence's sense of propriety. My daughter was a bit of a snob, and she never forgave me for my chosen occupation. When Addy was born, Florence was determined to eradicate any trace of La Rue blood in her. She brought that child up in an antiseptic atmosphere of respectability. Why, the child was almost eleven before I ever set eyes on her." There was a long, silent pause, and Mac couldn't help but feel for Blackie. "You see, Mac," Blackie began softly, "I lost my only daughter's respect and love because of my past, and I'm not about to lose Addy because of it, too. That child means too much to me, Mac. I wouldn't do anything in this world to hurt her. And if she finds out about me..." Blackie's voice trailed off, and Mac thought he detected a bit of sadness in the ensuing silence, and something else: fear.

Mac decided it wasn't any of his business what Blackie chose to tell or not tell his granddaughter. That was between them, and Mac had a clear policy of never interfering in family business.

"Sounds fair to me," Mac said, deciding to chance what was obviously a sore subject. "Blackie, why didn't you tell me about Simpson House? You could have come to me, I would have given you the money."

"*Given* me the money," came Blackie's insulted reply. Mac could hear the contempt in the man's voice and bit back a smile. He'd forgotten how proud the old man was. Just like his own grandfather. Having Blackie around even for just a few days helped fill the void his grandfather's death had left. Mac hated to admit he was growing quite fond of Blackie, even if the man did drive him crazy.

"MacArthur Cole," Blackie said, his voice tinged with disgust. "Blackie La Rue never took a handout from anyone in his life, and he's not about to start now. I'm perfectly capable of making the money we need on my own."

"That's what I'm afraid of," Mac muttered dismally, praying Blackie didn't decide to go back into business—on his own.

"Now, what are *we* going to do about Addy?" Blackie inquired blithely.

"*We?*" Mac squirmed in his chair. He didn't like the sound of this. "What do you mean, 'we'? She's *your* granddaughter."

"True, true," Blackie responded with a hint of delight. "But if I remember correctly, we made a deal. You were not to tell anyone I was here, or why I was here, and that *includes* Addy. You can't tell her about me, or our little deal. Or that you even know me."

Mac frowned. What Blackie had said was true. Mac had given his word, and he wasn't about to go back on it. But that was before Miss Adeline Simpson showed up and threw a monkey wrench into the whole thing.

"But, Blackie, she's determined to find you," Mac said, his sense of doom growing stronger. "Worse, she wants me to help her."

"Why, that's perfect, my boy," Blackie insisted glee-fully, causing Mac's feet to hit the floor with a thud. "You can *pretend* you're helping her find me, when in fact, what you'll be doing is *keeping* her from finding me. You'll just have to keep her busy looking for me in all the wrong places, of course—"

"Of course," Mac inserted sourly.

"—then I can go about my business without worrying about running into her. It's really quite simple," Blackie declared, totally pleased with the entire scenario.

"Simple, huh?" Mac growled, wearily dragging a hand through his hair.

It wasn't in his nature to lie or be deceitful, particularly to a woman. It was clear Addy was deeply distressed about her grandfather, and Mac certainly didn't want to add to her concern. "Blackie," Mac began dubiously, "are you say-ing you want me to lie and deceive Adeline?"

Blackie chuckled softly. "You catch on quickly, my boy," Blackie praised. "Must be some of your grandfather's blood in you somewhere."

"Blackie, I don't like this one bit." The idea of taking advantage of Addy, particularly in her distressed state, was not something Mac found particularly appealing.

"Well, then, I guess we'll just have to call the whole thing off," Blackie threatened, knowing the effect his words would cause. "By the way, Mac, how much did you say the casino was losing?"

Damn! Blackie had him, and he knew it. Mac had to go along with him despite his displeasure. The casino was los-ing a bundle every day, money they could ill afford to lose. Mac had to find the culprit and Blackie was his only hope. If he didn't agree to Blackie's terms, he might as well forget about ever catching the person or persons responsible, and Mac couldn't do that. He had a responsibility to make sure the Parkland was run fairly, not to mention the added pressure of The Nevada Gaming Control Board. If any hint of impropriety was discovered at the casino, Mac could lose not only his gaming license, but his hotel and casino as well. He couldn't take a chance on that; too many people depended on him for their jobs and their livelihood. The Parkland was much too important. He was going to have to agree to Blackie's terms whether he liked it or not.

"Don't think of it as lying to her or deceiving her, Mac," Blackie rationalized, realizing the boy was having a conflict of conscience. "Just think of it as sort of doing your good deed for the day. You see, if you keep Addy occupied so I can continue, everyone will get what they want. *You'll get your culprit, I'll get the money we need to pay the taxes, and Addy will find me.*" There was a long pause. *"Eventually,"* Blackie added with a soft chuckle. "It's a foolproof plan, and quite simple, really."

"Simple," Mac grumbled, realizing he was between a rock and a hard place. Why did he have the feeling Blackie was enjoying himself immensely?

"I've got a couple of leads, Mac," Blackie added mysteriously, hoping to sway the obviously honest young man. "But I'm going to need a few days. You're going to have to keep Addy occupied and out of the casino until I put all the pieces together."

"Out of the casino?" Mac bellowed, absently fingering the scar on his cheek. This thing was getting more complicated by the minute. "And how, may I ask, am I supposed to do that? I'm supposed to be helping her find you. Don't you think it's going to be a bit suspicious if I tell her she can't come into the casino?"

"You'll think of something, my boy," Blackie said with a bit of humor. "I've got great confidence in your abilities. But remember, this is *my* granddaughter we're talking about. She's not some sophisticate from the big city. Addy's sweet, naive, and full of good old-fashioned midwestern values." Blackie shook his silver head, once again reminiscing about what could have been. "Why, she's never even been out of Muncie, poor thing."

Oh, what a pair he and his granddaughter could have made, Blackie thought. With Addy's sweet, angelic looks and his knowledge, they would have been an unbeatable combination. Oh, the marks they could have taken; the scams they could have run. Addy would have been a perfect foil. It would have been such fun. Alas, it wasn't to be.

His daughter, Florence, had instilled different values in Adeline, and in the process, she had stripped the young girl of any spirit or adventure. The poor child's individuality had been squashed like a bug under a rug.

Fun was a disgraceful word, something to be avoided at all costs. The child was raised to be respectful, serious and responsible. By the time Blackie had arrived in Muncie to take over the rearing of Addy, the damage had already been done.

Addy had been a quiet, serious child, far older and wiser than her years. It broke his heart to see his beautiful granddaughter a prisoner of her mother's conservative, respectable ways.

Addy never had a chance to be a child; never had a chance to dream or fantasize about life outside of Muncie. To Addy, Muncie *was* life. He had tried over the years to bring some fun and adventure into her life, and once or twice he had actually seen a mischievous twinkle shining in her beautiful green eyes, but it had quickly been replaced by a forlorn stare that broke his heart. If only he could give Addy a little bit of fun, let her know there was more to life than Muncie. He'd never given up trying. It never ceased to annoy him that his one and only grandchild was leading a life as exciting as a plate of day-old prunes.

"Blackie?" Mac hesitated, wondering if he should tell him about Adeline's marriage proposal. "I think there's something else you should know about?"

"What?"

"Addy thinks you've come to Vegas to try and gamble the money you need to pay the taxes. She wants to find you to tell you it's not necessary. Claims she's going to have the money you need in a few days."

Blackie's silver brows drew together and he tapped his silver-handled cane. "Where on earth did the child get that kind of money?"

"Seems some guy named Parsnips has proposed marriage. He promised Addy he'd give her the money to pay the taxes on Simpson House if she married him."

"He *what*!" Blackie bellowed, causing Mac to pull the phone away from his ear in order to prevent permanent hearing loss. "Why, that pompous bag of wind! Thinks he's good enough for my Addy, why, he's not fit to spit-shine her shoes! Florence handpicked Pernall for Addy when she was just a child. She wanted Addy to make a good marriage, and Pernall was the best thing available in Muncie. His family's in banking, and he's been sniffing around that poor girl since he was a pup. Through the years I've managed to keep the man at bay, but now... Why on earth would she even consider marrying that hapless bag of wind?" Blackie asked to no one in particular.

"I think to help you out of a bad spot," Mac replied softly.

"Help me? Help me!" Blackie was thoroughly indignant. "The day hasn't arrived yet when Blackie La Rue needs anyone's help," he huffed, clearly insulted.

"So what about this Parsnips fellow?" Mac couldn't help but inquire, his curiosity getting the best of him.

Blackie sniffed loudly as if something foul was in the air. "The man's a jackass," Blackie pronounced with conviction. "His idea of fun is sitting around gloating over the bank's latest foreclosure notices. Thinks because he runs the town's largest bank he can have anything he wants. Well, I've got news for him. He's not getting his hands on my Addy, not if I have anything to say about it."

Mac stifled a smile. "I take it you don't ... ah ... care for Parsnips?"

"If boredom was a capital offense, Mac, that man would have been hung years ago. Marry my Addy, indeed! Who does he think he is?"

Before Mac could answer, Blackie rushed on. "Now, listen, Mac, this changes everything. I just need a couple of days and all of our problems will be solved. If Addy knows I've got the money to pay the taxes, then she won't even have to consider marrying that boring little bushwhacker. *She can't go back home until I have the money, and I won't have the money until I catch the casino culprit.* Mac, you need me and I need you. *I'll* find your culprit, if *you* promise to keep Addy here and busy until I do. Her whole future depends on it. I'm afraid if she goes back, Pernall will talk her into marrying him for her own good. I'll help you, if you help me. Is it a deal?"

Mac's feet hit the floor with a thud. "Blackie, how on earth do you expect—"

"Is it a deal?" Blackie repeated more sternly, knowing the clock was ticking.

Mac sighed in resignation. "It's a deal."

"Good. You have to keep Addy busy and out of the casino, and—"

"But how am I supposed to keep her out of the casino?" Mac inquired again, realizing this thing was growing larger with each passing moment. "*I'm supposed to be helping her find you,* remember?"

"*Lie,*" Blackie snapped, totally without conscience. "It's for her own good, Mac. Someday she'll thank me for it.

You're a smart boy, you'll think of something. Look, I've got to run. I'll talk to you in a few days."

"Blackie? Blackie?" The phone went dead in his hand and Mac swore softly. This situation had turned out to be much more complicated than he had ever envisioned. Somehow, someway, he was going to have to find Miss Adeline Simpson from Muncie, Indiana, convince her that he had had a sudden change of heart and was now willing to help her locate her grandfather, then keep her busy and out of the casino without making her suspicious! The idea of deceiving Addy was particularly distasteful, but, Mac rationalized, like Blackie said, it was for her own good. In the end, she would be able to find her grandfather and save Simpson House.

As for marrying Pernall, the thought caused Mac to frown. Why did it bother him? he wondered. He barely knew the woman, yet he found himself desperately wanting to know more about her. It had been a long, long time since he'd been so intrigued by a lady. The idea of spending time with Addy was becoming more appealing by the moment. Now, all he had to do was find her. No easy task, he realized, particularly since he had no idea where she had gone.

The red phone on Mac's desk began to peal urgently and he snatched it up quickly. That phone was used only when there was trouble down on the floor. The last thing he needed today was more trouble.

Mac listened quietly for a moment. With an oath of disgust, he slammed the receiver down. At least one of his problems was solved. He'd just found Addy. Or rather, his security department had!

Chapter Three

The moment Mac stepped out of his private elevator onto the casino floor he saw them; even if he hadn't seen them, he would have *heard* them. Half of Nevada could have heard the commotion.

Mac pushed his way through the assembled crowd of on-lookers. His eyes sprung wide open as his gaze landed on Addy. She was flanked on either side by one of the casino's burly security guards, each of whom had a rather secure hold on her arm, much to her displeasure, if the tone and volume of her voice was any indication.

From the look on Addy's face, he wasn't quite sure who was in more danger at the moment—the guards or Addy. She was giving both men a verbal dressing-down, pelting them with words and clearly unimpressed with either their size or their position.

Both looked like schoolboys caught playing hooky, Mac thought humorously. He had a feeling the feisty Miss Adeline Simpson could hold her own with anyone, even the casino's finest. No doubt she took after her grandfather.

"What's going on?" Mac asked, pushing his way closer. Neither Addy, the guards nor the large angry man Addy was now dressing down paid the least bit of attention to him.

Sighing heavily, Mac tried again. "What's going on?" he asked a bit more loudly.

For the second time that day, Addy whirled at the sound of Mac's voice. A few moments ago she was so furious with him she would have gladly said it would be a pleasure never to see his weather-beaten face again. But at the moment, he was the most welcome sight in the world.

"Mac," she breathed, her relief clearly evident in her face.

"Mr. Cole," the guards echoed in unison, looking clearly uncomfortable. The large angry man in the Stetson, who Mac recognized as a regular casino patron named Harry, also turned his attention toward Mac. The assembled crowd all began speaking at once, each one trying to drown out the other. The effect was a loud, confused din.

"Wait a minute," Mac bellowed, holding up his hand. "One at a time." He glanced at Addy. Her chin lifted stubbornly, and she glared at the guards who continued to hold her in check.

"These two...*gentlemen*," she said sarcastically, "think I'm...I'm..." She glanced up at Mac and flushed crimson. Straightening her frame, she threw back her shoulders and held her head high. "Would you please tell these men that I'm *not* what they think I am, and I *wasn't* doing whatever it is they think I was doing." Her words were as sharp as a rapier, causing Mac to look at her quizzically. He didn't have a clue as to what she was trying to tell him. Deciphering cryptic messages had never been his forte. Whatever was wrong had clearly ruffled her feathers, but she was paddling like crazy, trying to stay afloat.

"You wanna run that by me again?" he asked, looking at Addy for some help.

Her lips compressed in vexation. She would die of mortification if she had to tell Mac right here, in front of the Lord and all these people, just exactly what these guards thought she *was*, and what they thought she'd been doing.

"Boss?" One of the guards looked beseechingly at Mac. "Maybe I can straighten this out." He let go of Addy's arm and took a step back, motioning for Mac to join him.

Quizzically Mac followed, bending down so the guard could whisper in his ear. With a bemused smile, Mac straightened and headed back toward Addy.

"All right, boys," Mac said, "I think I can handle this from here."

Addy yanked herself free of the remaining guard with such force she nearly tumbled backward. Mac caught her by the shoulders, steadying her.

Mac casually dropped an arm around Addy. He had to handle this quickly and judiciously. Harry was a very good customer of the Parkland, and Mac didn't want to do anything to offend him. On the other hand, he didn't want to upset Addy any more than she already was. From the look on her face, he had a feeling her temper was about to blow.

"Harry," Mac began with a reassuring smile on his face, "I think there's been a misunderstanding."

"No, sir, Mac, I don't think so." Harry knocked his Stetson back farther on his head and grunted. "I understood *real* good." He flashed them a toothy, wicked grin. "Why, this pretty little gal sat down right next to me over yonder at that table. She was looking so distressed, I asked her if there was something I could do to ease her mind." He glanced at Addy, who continued to glare at him. "That's when she told me she was *looking for a man*. Even though she's a bit scrawny for my tastes—"

"Scrawny!" Addy fumed, balling her hands into fists and taking a step closer to the much larger man.

Oh, Lord, Mac thought with a sigh, tightening his arm around Addy's shoulders and holding her in check. Didn't the woman recognize a dangerous situation when she saw one?

"Anyway," Harry went on, "scrawny as she is, I figured, what the hey, if she's looking for a man, well, you know me, Mac." Harry reached up and scratched his eyebrow, grinning sheepishly. "My momma always taught me to oblige a lady in distress. And when this little lady approached me, I mean—who was I to argue? If she was looking for a man, I was just going to help the poor little thing out." Harry flashed Mac a wink. "If you know what I mean?"

"Poor little thing!" With a murderous glint in her eye, Addy tried to step toward Harry, but Mac held on tight. "Let go of me," she snarled, trying to pull away from him. Realizing she was outweighed, she turned her venom on hapless Harry.

"You, sir," she snapped, inhaling a deep gust of air through her flared nose. Harry took a cautious step backward. "Wouldn't know a *lady* if she walked up and bit you on your—"

"Addy!" Mac gasped, turning to her in surprise and trying to bank down a smile.

"—and," Addy continued, ignoring Mac, "it would be a cold day in hell when I would have the need to be rescued by the likes of you! Poor little thing, indeed!"

"Addy!" Mac glanced at her wildly. He was sorely tempted to clamp his hand over her mouth to quiet her, but he had no doubt she would take pleasure in sinking her beautiful pearly teeth right into his skin.

"That's all right, Mac," Harry said, obviously enjoying Addy's pique of anger. "I've got to admit, she may be scrawny, but she sure's got a spunky streak," Harry conceded, cocking his head to inspect Addy as if she were one of his prize cattle. "Kind of like that in a lady, Mac. I surely do. Ain't seen a filly with this much spunk in many a moon. We were just about to get better acquainted, when your guards came moseying along." Harry leaned forward and lowered his voice. "Guess they didn't take too kindly to her soliciting the customers."

"Soliciting!" Addy broke free of Mac and charged toward Harry, who reared back in surprise. From the look on his face, it was clear he thought Addy had just a bit too much spunk for his taste.

"Addy," Mac growled, grabbing her by the back of her blouse and reining her in. He dropped his arm across her shoulder and tightened his fingers around her so he'd be certain she'd stay put.

"Harry," Mac said smoothly, ignoring Addy's fury. He'd deal with her later. Right now he had to appease Harry. "I'm afraid you did misunderstand. You see, this lady here is...is—" Mac thought quickly "—*my cousin from Indiana.* She's, ah, just visiting from the Midwest, and the man she was looking for was me. I was supposed to meet her down here, but I'm afraid I got tied up with some pressing business and was detained upstairs. Isn't that right, *Cousin Adeline*?" Mac turned to her. Their eyes met and held. Belligerent green eyes clashed with large patient blue ones. His fingers tightened on her shoulder, and Addy became totally unnerved by his closeness. For a fraction of a moment, Addy was so ensnared by Mac's gaze, she almost forgot what he was saying.

"Isn't that right, *Cousin* Addy?" Mac prompted, squeezing her shoulder gently and bringing her out of her reverie.

Cousin, indeed! Blinking twice, she glared at him. How dare Mac stand here and tell such bold-faced lies? And to

make matters worse, he expected *her* to confirm his ficti-
tious story! Why didn't he just tell this boorish man he was
rude, pompous and an idiot to boot! She was unaccus-
tomed to telling lies. But obviously Mac was a man accus-
tomed to altering the truth to suit the situation. It was
something she'd have to keep in mind. *Cousin, indeed!*

"*Cousin* Addy," Mac growled, nudging her shoulder as
if willing the words out of her. His blue eyes darkened, and
for a moment Addy felt a flash of fear. She'd back up his
story—for the moment—but when she got MacArthur Cole
alone...

"That's right," Adeline agreed tightly, almost choking on
the feeble lie.

"Lordy, Lordy," Harry's face turned beet red. Remov-
ing his hat, he shook his head. "I'm rightly sorry, Mac. I
truly am. Why I never—I mean—I certainly wouldn't
have—" He hung his head. "Shucks, Mac, I meant no
harm. But when a pretty little thing approaches me and tells
me she's looking for a man, well..." His voice trailed off
and he grinned sheepishly. "I do apologize though,
ma'am," he said to Addy, who continued to glare at him.
"No harm intended."

"That's all right, Harry," Mac said before Addy could
open her mouth. He had to get Addy out of here before she
erupted and spilled the beans about his little white lie. "No
harm taken," Mac assured the man as he steered Addy
around in the opposite direction in order to make a quick,
smooth getaway. "I'm sorry for the commotion," Mac said
over his shoulder as he nudged Addy forward. "Tell you
what, Harry, talk to Jack in the Pit and tell him I said to
make reservations for dinner and the show tonight—on
me."

Harry brightened considerably. "Why, thank you, Mac,"
Harry called to their retreating backs. "That's right neigh-

borly of you. And I hope you and your cousin have a real nice visit.''

Keeping her head down and her mouth shut, Addy allowed Mac to guide her through the crowded casino. She waited until they were at a secluded spot near a bank of telephones before whirling on him.

''You told that man I was your cousin.''

''I did,'' Mac confirmed without a hint of remorse. He grinned down at her, only infuriating her further.

''But you *lied*,'' she cried.

''I did that, too,'' Mac agreed, causing her anxiety level to rise as he continued to urge her forward with a hand to her back. Addy came to an abrupt halt. Refusing to budge, she dug her heels into the plush carpet and turned to Mac, fire blazing from her eyes.

''Mr. Cole,'' she fumed. ''It wasn't enough that you lied to that man, but you made *me* lie to him, too. I don't know what kind of morals you people have here in Nevada, but back home in—''

''Addy.'' The tone of his voice stopped her cold. It was so soft, so quiet, she glanced up at him in surprise. ''If you'd just calm down a bit, I'd explain.''

She lifted her chin. ''Explain,'' she ordered, knowing there was no satisfactory explanation he could give for his behavior.

Mac dragged a hand through his hair, trying to hide his exasperation. ''Addy,'' he began carefully, dropping his hands to her shoulders to hold her in place, totally unaware of the discord his touch was causing her. ''Listen to me. This is Las Vegas, not Muncie. You just can't go around sidling up to strange men and announce you're looking for a man.''

''But I *am*,'' she insisted, paying no mind to his exasperation. She had some exasperation of her own to vent. ''And I told you before, if *you're* not going to help me find my grandfather, then I'll find someone who will.''

"Addy—" Mac stopped abruptly, bending down to peer at her. He was examining her as one might examine a bug under a microscope. She squirmed uncomfortably, automatically lifting a hand to her warm neck.

"What's wrong?" she asked, suddenly alarmed by the look on his face.

Mac's frown deepened. Curious, he leaned down to inspect her more closely. "Why is your neck all splotchy? It's the most peculiar shade of berry red I've ever seen." He tried not to grin, but couldn't help it. He was certain she had no idea just how attractive she was—with or without her dander up. Berry splotches or not.

Addy groaned softly, damning the telltale flush, which she knew was getting redder and warmer by the minute. "I...I...every time I tell a lie, my neck gets—stop laughing, MacArthur," she snapped, furious that the man found this whole situation so amusing. "This is all your fault," she accused, poking one slender finger into the middle of his broad chest.

"My fault!" Mac bellowed. "How the hell is this my fault? *You're* the one who approached that guy, not me. *You're* the one the guards mistook for a *hooker*." Mac leaned back on his heels, crossed his arms across his chest and grinned down at her, totally bemused by the heated flush that continued to cover not only her neck, but her face as well. "And, Miss Simpson, if I recall correctly, if it wasn't for *me*, right now you'd be sitting in the Clark County Jail trying to explain to an officer of the law just exactly what you *were* doing. It seems to me you should be thanking me, not chastising me."

"Thanking you!" Addy's body tightened in fury as she met his challenging gaze without flinching. "You have a lot of nerve," she accused, glaring up into his amused face. She didn't find anything particularly funny about this situation, and the fact that he did only irritated her more. "If it wasn't for *you*, I wouldn't have had to go around approaching strange men, or resort to telling lies. First you tell me you'll help me find my grandfather, then you tell me you won't. Not only can you not make up your mind, but apparently you can't tell the truth, either!''

"Ow, that hurt." Mac drew back, doing his best to look offended. "Would you have preferred that I let the guards haul you away and let Harry go on thinking you were a—''

"No!" Addy glared at him, annoyed by his logic. He was right—at least partially, and the thought galled her to no end.

"I think the least I deserve is a thank-you." Mac smiled. "And an apology."

"Apology!"

"At the least," Mac assured her, his grin widening.

"Aughhh," Addy growled, turning on her heel and marching away from him.

"Does this man I don't get my apology?" Mac called, his voice lilting with mischief. He followed behind her.

Addy ignored him and kept on walking. She couldn't waste time arguing with Mac. She had far more important things to do and little time to do them. She had to find a place to stay, get settled and locate her grandfather—with or without MacArthur Cole's help.

"Where are you going, now?" Mac asked, coming up behind her. He had no intention of letting her go—anywhere. But for the moment, he was having fun with her. Miss Adeline Simpson was quite a sight when she was riled. He was growing more intrigued by the moment. He had a feeling spending time with Miss Adeline Simpson from Muncie, Indiana, was going to be a pleasure.

Sighing in mock despair, Addy continued to ignore him, despite the fact that he was dogging her heels like a starving puppy. Why didn't the man just leave her alone? Up in his office he couldn't seem to get rid of her fast enough. Now, he couldn't seem to leave her alone. Why didn't he just make up his mind?

MacArthur Cole was quickly becoming a problem. And she didn't need another problem right now. She needed to put some space and some distance between them so she could concentrate on the matter at hand. She couldn't afford to have her attention diverted by anyone, not even the intensely masculine MacArthur Cole.

Addy had known from the moment she had walked into his office that there was something different, special about Mac. He stirred up certain feminine feelings that were totally disconcerting, not to mention downright alarming.

"Adeline," Mac said in a voice loud enough to cause several people to look at him curiously. "Where are you going?" he repeated, ignoring the fact that they were on the verge of creating another scene. Addy sighed.

"I'm going to find a room, not that it's any of your business," she snapped. She kept on walking, heading toward the registration desk, and stepping into the line of people that had formed there.

"There's no point in waiting in line," Mac said. "All the rooms in the hotel are booked." He looked decidedly pleased, Addy thought, wondering why the man had the ability to annoy her so.

"Then I'll go to another hotel." She pivoted abruptly, heading in the opposite direction toward the bellman's desk, where she had stored her bags.

"Don't bother," Mac said casually, following close behind her. "Without a reservation, you're not going to be able to find a room anywhere in this town. This is the biggest weekend of the year, Addy. Every single hotel room is booked because of the heavyweight fight Saturday night." He smiled. "The only available sleeping place is probably a park bench."

"Then I'll sleep on a park bench," Addy called over her shoulder, causing Mac to heave a weary sigh. She was stubborn all right. "I don't care where I have to sleep," she called. "I'm not leaving this town until I find my grandfather."

"Addy." He caught her elbow and brought her to a halt. "Wait a minute."

She whirled to face him, stunned to find him standing directly behind her. He was so close she could see the thick inky richness of his lashes. It caused her heart to skip a beat. The warmth of his hand radiated through her, causing her to shiver. Must the man keep touching her? It caused her nervous system to wail in alarm. She wasn't used to this type of casual touching, particularly from a male—a male she found totally disconcerting. His intense masculinity made her nervous.

"I don't have time to wait," she snapped, trying unsuccessfully to break free of him. "I told you, I have to find my grandfather."

"Well, you're going about it all wrong," he announced confidently, knowing it would get her dander up. It did.

Addy turned slowly. Fire darkened her eyes and she glared up at him. "And I suppose *you're* an expert at finding people?" she challenged, placing her hands on her hips. "I thought you told me this was a casino, *not a lost and found*. Besides, what makes you think I'd take any advice from you? *You* can't even make up your mind," she accused, knowing it was a low blow, but beyond caring. "One minute you say you'll help me, and the next you say you won't. What makes you think I'd believe anything you say?"

This was turning out to be much more complicated than she'd ever imagined. Before she left home, she hadn't given any thought to securing a room reservation or formulating a plan. She'd been so upset by her grandfather's uncharacteristic disappearance, her immediate response was to hop the first plane and find him. Too bad she hadn't given more thought to *how* she was going to find him.

"Well, Addy, you can believe this. You can't just start roaming the streets of Las Vegas approaching every strange man you see. Like I said, this isn't Muncie, Addy. You're likely to find yourself in a heap of trouble if you go about things that way."

"You've no need to worry about me, Mr. Cole," Addy said coolly. "I assure you I can take care of myself."

"Take care of myself, huh?" he repeated, chuckling softly. "Addy, what do you plan to do the next time you get in a jam? Like I said, this isn't Muncie. First of all, you have no place to stay, and no reservations. Other than me, you don't know anyone else in the entire state, let alone the city. How much money do you have?" he asked abruptly, startling her into answering.

"About a hundred dollars," she blurted before realizing she was obliging his nosiness.

"A hundred dollars." Mac shook his head. "I don't know how to tell you this, Addy, but at the rate you're going, you'll be lucky not to be locked up on a vagrancy charge by midnight. Then what? How do you think Parsnips would take it if he knew his bride-to-be had been caught soliciting in a casino, and then arrested for vagrancy? My, my, I'll bet that would make interesting reading for the folks back home."

Merciful Heaven! Just the thought of Pernall finding out about where she was, no less her reasons for being in Vegas, was enough to make her shudder. But she wasn't about to admit it to Mac.

"I suppose you've got a better idea?"

"Maybe," he said with an evasive grin.

"'Maybe' is not an answer," she snapped. "I told you, I don't have time to waste arguing with you. I've got more important things to do. Besides, you needn't concern yourself with my welfare. I'm sure I'll be just fine.''

''I certainly can't let you go wandering around the streets of Las Vegas all by yourself. Who knows the kind of trouble you could get into? You can't even find a room. How on earth do you expect to find your grandfather?''

Addy closed her eyes for a moment, praying for some of Great-Grandmother Simpson's patience. Unfortunately, none was forthcoming. How could locating one small elderly gentleman turn out to be so difficult? she wondered, feeling suddenly overwhelmed.

A thought suddenly occurred to Addy and she opened her eyes, looking at Mac suspiciously. Why was he trying to be so helpful all of a sudden? She had a feeling he was up to something—what, she didn't know. At the moment, she wasn't sure she wanted to know.

''Upstairs you told me you couldn't help me. Why the sudden change of heart?'' she asked, watching him carefully. ''Why?'' she repeated suspiciously, causing Mac to grin.

''Let's just say I'm a Good Samaritan.''

''Let's not.''

Mac drew back, doing his best to look offended. ''Are you insinuating I wouldn't come to the aid of a damsel in distress?''

''The only distress I'm having at the moment is you,'' Addy said, sidestepping around him.

''Why are you giving me such a hard time?'' Mac asked, grabbing her hand to stop her before she could issue a protest. ''Here I am, trying to help you out, and all you keep doing is insulting me. If I remember correctly, you once told me that people in Muncie treated others with regard and respect. Does that apply to everyone but me?'' He looked at her thoughtfully and Addy immediately felt a rush of remorse.

What on earth was the matter with her? It was unlike her to be so rude or so ungrateful to someone. Mac had helped her out of a jam, and he was trying to be kind in his own intriguing way, but all she had been doing was insulting him. How ungrateful she must seem! It certainly wasn't his fault her grandfather had up and disappeared. And it also wasn't his fault that she hadn't planned ahead or thought things through and now found herself without a place to lay her head, let alone a plan to find her grandfather. Those were her problems, and yet here she was, taking out her frustrations on him.

Perhaps it was because of her unusual reactions to him. Just being around Mac made her acutely aware of her own femininity, something she'd *never* been aware of—until now. Mac had the ability with just a look or just a touch to make her feel like the most desirable creature around. It was those blasted eyes of his, she decided. But that was not his fault, either. He was probably totally unaware of the reaction he had on her. It wasn't his fault he was so darn appealing! She had absolutely no reason to be so rude to him.

"I'm sorry," she said softly, dropping her gaze and biting her trembling lips. She slowly lifted her eyes to his. "It's just . . . I'm just so worried about Grandpa. This is so unlike him, Mac. He's not a young man anymore, and with each passing moment, my anxiety increases."

"I know," Mac said gently, tipping her chin up. "But you're not going to find him if you go off half-cocked without a plan. Roaming around from casino to casino isn't going to get you anywhere. For all you know you could be going in circles, missing him at every turn. You've got to have a plan, Addy."

"I know," she glumly admitted.

"And before you can even begin to formulate a plan, you've got to have a place to stay."

"I know that, too," she said forlornly, wishing she hadn't been so hasty in rushing off. It wasn't like her; she was usually logical and methodical about things. But then again, her grandfather had never disappeared before. He meant so much to her, locating him had been of utmost importance, all of the other things had simply never occurred to her.

"Addy, if you're willing to calm down a bit and listen to me, I think I've got a solution to both of your problems."

Addy glanced up at Mac in surprise. "Both problems?"

"The first thing we have to do is get you settled. The hotels are out. You won't find a room anywhere, not even with my pull. But if you're willing to trust me, I think I have a place for you to stay." His gaze met hers, and Addy saw something in his eyes she didn't quite understand. Despite the spaciousness of the casino, and all the people milling about, Addy was suddenly and acutely aware of Mac's presence. It was as if they were the only two people in the room. Entranced by his gaze, Addy stood there, staring at him, allowing his eyes to soothe and calm her fears. Mac was asking her to trust him. Trust him? Her thoughts spun. How on earth could she trust a man she had known barely two hours and who had done nothing but change his mind and lie? Hardly sterling qualities to judge a character by.

On the other hand, Addy reasoned, under the circumstances, she really had no choice. What else could she do *but* trust the man if she ever wanted to find her grandfather? One look at the huge complex of glittering casinos that lined the strip told her searching on her own would be a futile effort. She could search until the cows came home and never find her grandfather. But maybe, just maybe, with Mac's help and knowledge of the town, she might be able to accomplish her mission. But it meant trusting him. Could she do it?

Addy's usual cautiousness seemed to dissolve. She suddenly realized she couldn't afford *not* to trust Mac. She had no choice. He was her only hope, and it was about time she swallowed her stubborn pride and admitted it. She needed MacArthur Cole whether she liked it or not.

And at the moment, she didn't have the pleasure of pondering what his reasons were for changing his mind. Hadn't her mother always told her not to look a gift horse in the mouth?

"Addy?" Mac said softly, his gaze still holding hers. What was it about his eyes? she wondered. There was a gentleness, a kindness that might be overlooked had someone not bothered to look beyond his appearance. Outwardly he looked like an intimidating man, but inside, there was a man of humor and compassion. A man of caring and concern.

It was surprising how much she had learned about Mac in just a couple of hours. Perhaps that's why, instinctively, she felt she could trust him. The length of time she had known him suddenly didn't matter. What mattered were her own gut instincts, instincts that had yet to fail her in all her twenty-three years.

"Addy?" he prompted, reaching down to take her hands in his. His hands were large, engulfing hers in a reassuring embrace.

Deciding to throw caution, and perhaps common sense, to the wind, Addy smiled. "I . . . I'll trust you," she said tentatively, more unnerved by his touch than what she was promising to do.

"Great." Mac grinned down at her. His beautiful blue eyes seemed to come alive when he smiled. "First things first. We've got to find you a place to stay. I know just the place."

"The park bench?" Addy asked cautiously, causing Mac to chuckle.

"No. What I've got in mind is a bit more comfortable. Come on, let's get your bags and I'll show you."

Curious, yet realizing she didn't have much choice in the matter, Addy allowed Mac to collect her lone piece of luggage and lead her out to the parking lot.

She hesitated a moment when they reached his car. "Mac?"

He glanced at her. "What?"

"Wh . . . where are we going?"

His brows wiggled in mischief, and a smile slanted his lips. "I'm taking you home, of course."

Chapter Four

Home!" Addy cried, trying to lunge for her suitcase and grab it from Mac. He refused to let it go. He simply swung it into the back seat and opened the car door for her. Addy kept staring at him in wooden silence. "Whose home?" she finally managed to get out, knowing the answer before he even opened his mouth.

"My home," Mac replied smoothly. Taking advantage of her shock, Mac ushered her into the car and slammed the door soundly shut. He hurriedly walked around the car and climbed behind the wheel. "Do you have a problem with that?" he asked, knowing just by the stunned expression on her face it was a major problem. He couldn't help but find it amusing.

"Addy?" Quickly bringing the car to life, Mac pulled away from the casino, watching as Addy craned her neck to watch the hotel fade into the distance. "Are you worried about coming home with me?" He was studying her carefully so she knew she couldn't lie. How could she tell him that she couldn't possibly stay at his house?

"Worried?" she repeated, stalling for time.

"Yes, worried. Listen, you've got nothing to fear from me. Besides, Hildy will be there. She's *always* there. She'll vouch for my character. We'll be properly chaperoned so you won't have to worry about what Parsnips will think."

Addy swallowed hard. That's exactly what she was doing. Merciful Heaven. How on earth would she ever be able to explain to Pernall that she was sharing a house with a man she not only wasn't married or related to, but a man she had barely known two hours? Lord, she couldn't think about that now. She'd think about it later. Right now she had more pressing problems to occupy her thoughts.

"Who is Hildy?" she asked, trying not to let her worry show.

Mac chuckled softly. "Well, she's *supposed* to be my housekeeper, but I think someone forgot to tell her. Actually, she's really part of the family. She's been with me and my sister, Rosie, for years."

She glanced at him in surprise. "*You* have a sister?"

Mac's eyes twinkled in merriment. "Did you think I was hatched from an egg? Don't you think someone like me could have a sister?"

Addy flushed. "No, that's not quite what I meant. I'm just . . . surprised."

"Rosie's Chief of Security at the Parkland. She's in Hawaii right now on vacation." He failed to add that because of their current problems, he had to practically force Rosie to go on her trip. He had finally convinced her there was nothing she could do. "If I've managed to live with two women all my life, I can't see how one more is going to make any difference."

Addy stared at him. MacArthur Cole was a man full of surprises. She would have imagined he'd live in a swinging bachelor pad in the heart of the glittering city. Now, she learned he apparently shared a home on the outskirts of town with his sister and a housekeeper. Interesting.

"You'll like Hildy," Mac offered. "You two have a lot in common."

"We do?"

"Yes, she's crotchety, moody and has a terrible temper." Mac grinned. "I'd say that's a lot in common."

Before Addy could open her mouth to issue an angry retort, Mac reached out and covered her hand with his. "I was just kidding, so don't get your dander up. What do you say we call a truce? I'll help you find your grandfather, if you promise to try to be nice to me. I'm really a very pleasant person once you get to know me. Ask anyone," he suggested, causing Addy to frown.

"I don't *know* anyone," she reminded him glumly.

"You know me," Mac said. "And for now, that's enough. So how about it? Is it a deal?" he asked. "Are we going to call a truce?"

"Are you really going to help me find my grandfather?"

"That's what I said." He glanced over at her. "I'm not saying it's going to be easy. But we'll give it our best shot."

"It's a truce then," Addy said, suddenly feeling better about the whole situation.

"So tell me, why didn't Parsnips come with you to help look for your grandfather?"

Addy squirmed in her seat, trying to figure out how to answer his question without telling another lie. She decided to settle on the truth. "Pernall doesn't know I'm here."

Mac glanced at her. "You mean you just took off?"

Addy nodded glumly, causing Mac to smile. "When I realized Grandpa was gone, I had no choice. I knew if I told Pernall he'd have a fit. He and Grandpa don't get on very—" Addy stopped abruptly, realizing she had revealed more than she meant to.

"This guy and your grandpa don't what?" Mac prompted, wanting to hear more.

Addy glanced down at her folded hands. "Don't get on very well," she admitted.

"What's going to happen when Parsnips discovers you left without telling him?"

"I'm hoping he won't find out," she said with a long sigh. "I'll probably be home before he even realizes I'm gone."

Mac frowned, not understanding this one bit. "How could he not realize you're gone? I thought you two were engaged?"

"Well, not officially. He's proposed, but I'm supposed to be thinking it over."

"Even so, don't you see him or talk to him every day?" Mac couldn't imagine having a woman like Addy and letting a day go by without hearing her voice or seeing her beautiful face.

"No," she admitted. "Pernall works at the bank during the week and needs his rest. We have a standing date every Saturday evening."

"Needs his rest?" Mac repeated dumbfounded. "How old is this guy?" he asked. "And how long have you been seeing him?" This was a very strange relationship, Mac decided. No wonder Blackie didn't like Parsnips.

"A few years older than I am, and since we were children," she answered, deciding the direct approach was the best. "Why are you so curious about Pernall?" she inquired, suddenly testy at his interrogation.

"Just nosy, I guess," Mac said, not wanting to admit he was checking out his competition. If Parsnips didn't know what a jewel Miss Adeline Simpson was, he certainly wasn't about to point it out to the man. "How the hell can you get to know someone if you see him only once a week? How much do you *really* know about this guy?" Mac asked.

"Enough to know he's good company, pleasant, and will make a good companion," Addy said defensively, wondering about Mac's intense interest all of a sudden.

"Good *companion*," Mac repeated, stunned. No wonder Blackie couldn't stand the man. Mac wasn't too fond of him himself, and he'd never even met him. "Addy, if it's companionship you're looking for, a dog would be much cheaper in the long run. That's certainly not a reason to marry someone."

"Mac," she said stiffly. "I don't think this is a subject we should be discussing. You really don't know anything about Pernall, or about me, for that matter."

"I'll bet I know more about you right now, after only a few hours, than Parsnips would know after a lifetime," Mac challenged.

Addy sat in stunned silence, realizing Mac was right. She'd done things, said things and behaved in ways she would never have dreamed of doing in front of Pernall. With Pernall, she'd always felt as if she had to live up to his high expectations. With Mac, she had no such worries. Despite her behavior today, or maybe because of it, Mac seemed to accept her just as she was.

"Here we are," Mac said, pulling down a long, narrow road that turned into a driveway. He brought the car to a halt outside a sprawling adobe-style ranch house that looked as if it went on forever. The house was set back on acres of land filled with towering palm trees with beautiful green fronds that whispered gently in the breeze. The landscape in Nevada was so different from Indiana. Different, but beautiful.

As Mac came around to help Addy out of the car, the front door of the house was thrown open. Addy turned in surprise, taken aback by the large woman filling the doorway. She wore a flowered-print housedress, a long white apron, black high-topped running shoes and a scowl.

"Where the devil have you been, boy?" she demanded, coming down the walk to snatch Addy's suitcase out of his hand. "You're late, lunch is getting cold, half the town is looking for you, and Rosie called from Hawaii. She said she's having a wonderful time but she needs you to wire her some money."

"Again," was Mac's reply before taking Addy's elbow and guiding her toward the front door. She was instantly curious about the woman in the running shoes. She had a feeling she had just met the infamous Hildy.

"Again," Hildy confirmed, swinging Addy's suitcase up as if it were a feather. "And the manager of the Parkland in Reno called, said the head of bookkeeping is threatening to quit unless you get someone up there to untangle that new-fangled computer you installed. Said if you don't, you'll have mutiny on your hands."

"Anything else?" Mac asked with a sigh.

"You're late," Hildy repeated, dropping the suitcase to the marble foyer floor. "And who's this you've got with you?" she asked, placing her hands on her hips and turning to measure Addy with her eyes.

"This," Mac said with a smile, "is Miss Adeline Simpson from Muncie, Indiana."

"Indiana, huh?" Hildy said, not quite done with her visual appraisal of Addy yet. "Was there once. Nice place. Are you hungry?" she asked without taking a breath.

Addy glanced at Mac. "Don't go looking at him," Hildy scolded. "That boy ain't got enough sense to feed himself, let alone a guest. You come along into the kitchen," she ordered, tugging on Addy's hand. "And you, MacArthur, go get this pretty little thing settled in Rosie's room. Then return those calls and come have something to eat." It wasn't a request but an order, Addy noted with a smile, amazed at the way Mac jumped to Hildy's instructions.

Without waiting for a response, Hildy steered Addy through the foyer and down a long hallway through a pair of swinging doors into the kitchen.

The kitchen was huge. Sun streamed in through the patio doors and danced on the sparkling clean room, which was decorated in shades of muted yellow. The fragrant smells of chicken assaulted her senses and Addy's stomach grumbled. She hadn't had a thing to eat all day. This morning she'd been too nervous about her first airplane ride to get down any breakfast, and on the plane, they served what they called lunch, but what she called "meat surprise." She didn't dare attempt to eat it, fearing it might try to eat her back. Now, her stomach rumbled ominously at the luscious smells filling the sunny kitchen.

"Park it over there, honey," Hildy said, indicating one of the bright-yellow cushioned chairs. "I'll get you something to eat." Turning her back, Hildy busied herself at the stove, ladling a plate high with chicken, mashed potatoes, gravy and her special three-bean salad.

"Now," Hildy said as she slapped the plate down in front of Addy. "You go on and eat before everything gets cold."

Addy did as she was told, aware that Hildy was watching her carefully.

"So, what's your story?" Hildy finally asked as she plucked a chicken leg off Addy's plate.

"Story?" Addy repeated between bites.

"MacArthur hasn't brought a woman home for as long as I can remember." She looked at Addy shrewdly. "You must be someone special. You're right pretty enough, naturally pretty without all that phony goop and stuff." Hildy reached out and touched Addy's hair. "That color looks real, too," she said warmly, smiling for the first time.

Addy nearly choked on her food. "It is real," she said. Addy lifted her napkin and wiped her mouth. She certainly didn't want to give Hildy the wrong impression. "Hildy," she began cautiously, wanting to set the record straight, "I'm afraid you've got the wrong idea about Mac and me. He's just helping me with a problem."

"Humph," Hildy said, tossing the chicken bone across the room, directly into the waste can. "That ain't nothing new. MacArthur is forever helping someone with something. So what's your story?" Hildy asked again, obviously not in the least bit concerned that it might not be any of her business.

Addy chuckled, liking the woman's directness. Hildy reminded her of her grandfather. Slowly Addy began recounting the story of how she came to Las Vegas and to Mac's casino.

"Well, honey," Hildy said, patting Addy's hand. "If anyone can find your grandpappy, MacArthur can. That boy knows everything and everyone in this town." Hildy paused for a moment, glancing at Addy shrewdly. "You a married lady?" Hildy asked with all the subtlety of a roaring freight train.

Addy laughed again. "No. I'm not." She failed to add that she was almost about to be engaged. Somehow she had a feeling Hildy wouldn't understand, and after her conversation with Mac about Pernall, she wasn't up to another long drawn-out interrogation.

"Hmm," was all Hildy said with a mischievous twinkle in her eye. "Well, honey, I wouldn't worry about your grandpa. If MacArthur said he'd help you, he will. Sometimes men can be dumb as jackasses, but you'll have to look long and hard before you find one as good as MacArthur." Hildy narrowed her gaze on Addy. "But if you ever tell him I said so, I'll deny it."

Addy and Hildy broke into laughter. Neither heard the door swing open.

"What's so funny?" Mac asked, taking a seat opposite Addy.

"None of your business," Hildy shot back with a scowl. She scooped up Addy's empty plate and flashed her a conspiratorial wink. "Now sit down here and hush or I'll make you eat your lunch cold."

After filling a plate for Mac, and refilling Addy's, Hildy joined them at the table. They ate in comfortable silence, although Addy was vividly aware of Mac's presence next to her. It didn't help that he kept following her with his eyes. She was suddenly no longer hungry.

"Hildy," Addy finally said, pushing her plate away, "that's the best fried chicken I've ever had."

"Course, it is," Hildy agreed. "It's my own recipe. Now, how about some homemade apple pie?"

Addy groaned softly. "I couldn't eat another bite." She stifled a yawn. It had been a long, tiring day, and now that she had eaten Addy was suddenly exhausted.

Hildy stood up and began to clear the table. Addy jumped to her feet. "Please, let me help you. It's the least I can do after that delicious meal."

Hildy shooed her away. "Been doing it myself for years. Don't like anyone messing in my kitchen. Gives me hives." She glanced at Addy. "You run along now. You look like you can use a little shut-eye." She turned to Mac, who was watching them curiously. "MacArthur," she barked, causing him to straighten. "Take Addy here and show her to her room. She looks beat."

"No, really," Addy protested, suddenly feeling uncomfortable in Mac's house and not knowing why. They had done everything to make her feel at home. There was no reason for her to be nervous. "I'm fine."

"You heard the lady," Mac said, getting to his feet. "Come on." Mac took her hand and led her out of the kitchen and down a long, narrow hallway that branched out to another wing of the house where four bedrooms were strategically laid out. Mac opened the door to one of the rooms at the far end of the hall. "This is Rosie's room. I'm sure you'll find everything you need. There's a connecting bathroom with a shower and a Jacuzzi. I've already put your bag in there, so you should find everything you need. If not, just holler."

"Mac," Addy said, looking up at him. "What about my grandfather?"

He took a step closer. For a moment she tensed, then saw the warmth and humor in his eyes and began to relax, remembering what Hildy had said about him.

"I thought you said you'd trust me," he reminded her, lifting a hand to stroke her hair. She shifted a bit, realizing her once-neat braid was now terribly askew because of the windblown ride to the house. Mac's touch was gentle and somehow endearing. It seemed almost intimate in a way she didn't quite understand.

"I . . . I . . ." She struggled to find her tongue, wondering why his nearness had the ability to rob her of speech. "I do," she finally managed to get out, trying to take a step back from him. He was too close to her, so close her senses spiraled in confusion. She could smell the faint scent of Mac's after-shave. It was a musky male aroma that made her dizzy. She could see the darkening of Mac's eyes as they narrowed and roamed slowly over her features, savoring each and every inch of her and making her feel as if she were something precious and special. Why did he have that ability, she wondered, so lost in her own thoughts she hadn't realized he'd taken another step closer.

"We'll find your grandfather," he said softly, "but there's something I think we need to get out of the way first." Lifting his hands, he gently cradled her face. His eyes slowly settled on her mouth, and Addy nervously licked her parched lips. "This has nothing to do with your grandfather, Parsnips or anything else, Miss Adeline Simpson. This has to do with you and me." Without giving her time to protest, Mac's mouth lowered over hers.

His mouth was warm, sweet and soft. Her pulse pounded loudly in her ears, reminding her of the rush of the tide. Wave after wave of warm sensations flooded her body, almost causing her legs to buckle.

Addy raised her hands to his chest in an effort to push him away, to stop this madness now, before it became too late, but Mac moved in closer. Sliding his hands down her back to encircle her waist, he pulled her closer until she was pressed against the warm, hard length of him. Her hands were trapped between their bodies, and she could feel the rapid beating of a heart, whose, she wasn't sure, nor did she care. Her mind was filled with only one thought. *Mac*.

Unbridled passion exploded within Addy. Never had one simple kiss ever evoked such intense feelings, such intense emotions.

Mac's gentle lips roamed over hers, taking, possessing, stamping her with his own brand. As her thoughts fragmented into thousands of little pieces, she forgot everything and everyone but Mac. Addy laced her arms around his neck, pressing her eager body even closer to his.

She had always wondered what it would feel like to have a man pull her into his arms and kiss her until she was nearly dizzy. Now she knew. This was the kind of kiss she had always dreamed about. Mac's lips moved over hers, demanding, giving. Parting her lips, she allowed Mac to take all that she offered, returning all that she had been given.

Mac tightened his arms around her, stunned by her slightness. Addy was so soft, so fragile, he had an instinctive urge to cherish and protect her. He'd imagined what she'd taste like, had, in fact, thought of little else since he'd laid eyes on her, but never anticipated the sweet satisfaction that would fill him body and soul once he'd held her in his arms. He was surprised by her response. He'd expected her to resist or at least to be stiff, but she was soft, pliable, giving. Her mouth accepted his, giving and taking with his own, seeking and demanding more. She fit naturally in his arms as if she'd been born to be there. Raw need rose up and caught him by surprise, knocking him senseless. Never had one woman, one kiss, stirred him so. His trembling matched hers as they discovered the hidden secrets of each other's mouths, mouths that clung together as one.

For as long as Mac could remember, he'd had to fight for everything he'd gotten. Now, with one kiss, he knew his greatest fight was yet to come. He wanted Addy, of that he was sure, and not just in his bed, but in his life and in his heart, as well. He knew instinctively she belonged to him, and that they belonged together. It wouldn't be easy. But then, nothing he'd ever wanted had been. That hadn't stopped him in the past, and it surely wouldn't stop him now.

Somehow, someway, during the next few days he was going to have to show sweet Adeline that she deserved more than marriage to a man who was kind and companionable; she deserved more than to marry a man simply because he bailed her out of a tight spot. She deserved so much more. Adeline deserved love. And Mac intended to give it to her. Now and forever.

All he had to do was convince her of it. No easy task, he realized. Dealing with such a proud, not to mention stubborn, woman was definitely going to be a challenge. An *exciting* challenge, he amended silently. He was used to the kind of women who came on strong and kept on coming. It was no secret he was an eligible bachelor and a prime target for all the women who saw only dollar signs when they looked at him. Funny, he had a feeling Addy didn't know, much less care, how much he was worth. She wasn't the type of woman to come on to anyone; she was the type to be coaxed and coddled. There was an air of old-fashioned goodness about her that was refreshing and exciting.

Slowly she withdrew from his arms, trying to shake free the cloud of desire that engulfed her. Mac kept his arms around her to steady her as her eyes slowly fluttered open. The feelings assaulting her were so strong, so powerful, she couldn't speak. In just a beat of a heart, in just a moment of time, her life and her world had been altered. She'd always been a practical woman who believed in practical things. Love and romance were frivolous words meant for others. Now she knew differently. Now she understood. To be held in Mac's arms, to feel the need and desire within her matched by his frightened yet awakened her, causing her to long for more. Now Addy suddenly understood what it meant to lose yourself in a man's arms, in a moment's madness.

But she also understood that a moment was not long enough. She wanted much more than a moment; she wanted a lifetime.

"Addy?" Mac's breath was ragged, his words soft and tender as a caress. Gently he ran his hands across her back, causing goose bumps to fly across her skin. "Now you know," he said quietly, looking deeply into her eyes. "Kindness and companionship are not enough for a woman like you. And I aim to prove it." With that, Mac turned and strode down the hall, leaving Addy staring openmouthed after him.

A woman like you.

His words echoed over and over in her mind as reality slammed her back down to earth. A woman like her. She knew exactly just what kind of woman she was, probably better than anyone. Long ago she had learned exactly what she was and what she could expect in life. She had also learned not to indulge herself in fanciful dreams. She was nothing if not a realist.

Mac was the kind of man who would go for a long-legged blonde with an hourglass figure. A woman who was as confident and secure in her femininity as Addy was insecure. To even think that a man like Mac would find her attractive was only leaving herself open for heartache.

Had one kiss robbed her of all memory? How could she have forgotten her hard-learned lessons so easily? Her mother had always told her no man would come calling for her looks. How could one kiss, one man, change something she had known all her life? It couldn't, Addy realized sadly.

Once again she was wishing for more and not appreciating what she had. Addy dropped her head guiltily. She shouldn't be having such thoughts about Mac when she was supposed to be thinking over the proposal of another man. Pernall was a good, kind man and would make a fine husband. She had to appreciate him and all of his qualities and not be wishing for something, or rather *someone*, she couldn't have.

Sighing heavily, Addy went into the bedroom, leaned against the door and closed her eyes. What was she doing? She couldn't afford to let her personal feelings for Mac grow. She had to remember why she had come here. She couldn't forget her purpose.

In all of her life she had never behaved the way she had today. But then again, she mused, she had never met anyone like MacArthur Cole before. There was something about him, something kind and wonderful and alluring that seemed to draw her to him.

From the moment she had entered his office, she had felt the pull of his magnetism. He had a way of looking at her that made her feel as if she were the only woman in the world. Addy sighed. It was a wonderful feeling, a feminine feeling. A feeling she had always wondered about. Now she knew how simply glorious it felt to have the sole attention of an attractive, alluring man.

When Mac had held her in his arms, for that brief moment she felt cherished and cared for.

What would it be like to be loved by a man like Mac? Adeline wondered. The thought caused an unexpected smile to curve her lips. *Mac.*

Her smile slowly faded as she mentally gave herself a shake. What on earth was wrong with her? There was no sense wasting time lamenting about something that could never be. Las Vegas was filled with the most beautiful women in the world, glamorous, sophisticated women. Why on earth would he be interested in *her*? She had nothing to offer a man like Mac.

She had involved him in her problem, and being as kind as Hildy assured her he was, it was only natural that he offer his assistance. He probably just didn't want her disrupting his patrons any further.

After undressing and climbing into bed, Addy turned over, trying to drive thoughts of Mac out of her head.

Pernall was a good man, she reminded herself, and she *had* promised she would seriously consider his marriage proposal. And Adeline was not one to go back on a promise. Closing her eyes, she seriously tried to think about what life with Pernall would be like. As her thoughts spun, not for the first time did Adeline wonder wistfully if perhaps there wasn't just a bit more to life than Muncie, Indiana, and Pernall.

Mac. He came unbidden back into her thoughts.

When he had kissed her, he had given her a precious gift. He had allowed her the pleasure of feeling something she'd never dared hope to feel. Just once, for one brief shining moment, Addy hadn't been thinking with her mind, but with her heart. She wanted to forever remember the touch of Mac's lips on hers; she wanted to remember the way her pulse seemed to jump at his nearness, the way his soft sweet breath buffeted against her skin. Addy knew she was going to cherish that special moment with Mac and hold it close to her heart—forever.

"Any coffee left?" Mac asked Hildy as he pushed through the swinging door into the kitchen. He pulled out a chair and sat down heavily. He'd been more shaken by Addy's kiss than he realized.

Hildy set a steaming cup down in front of him and watched him carefully. "All right, MacArthur," she said, pulling out the chair next to him. "Out with it."

Mac glanced up, trying to fight down a smile. "Out with what?" He should know better than to try to hide anything from Hildy. She could smell a problem a mile away.

"Don't play dumb, boy. At my age, I don't have time for such nonsense. What's bothering you?" She cocked her head and looked at him shrewdly. "Wouldn't have something to do with that pretty little blonde you brought home, would it?"

Mac glanced up at her and grinned from ear to ear. "If you know, why are you asking?"

"'Cause I'm nosy," she declared, rising to get her own cup of coffee. "Now, let's have it, before it eats a hole in your stomach."

"Hildy," he began slowly, not quite sure how to put into words what he was feeling. "Have you ever met someone, and right away, you knew—I mean almost immediately you realized—that . . . that . . . they were something special?"

"Sure did," she confirmed with a nod of her gray head. "First time I laid eyes on you, but don't let it go to your head." Hildy was quiet for a moment, watching Mac as he twisted his coffee mug around in his hands. "Now, why do I get the feeling that's not the kind of special you're talking about?"

"It's not," he confirmed, taking a sip of his coffee.

"Does she know?" Hildy asked, surprising him with her perceptiveness. Mac shook his head. "Well, that ain't too bright, son, unless of course the lady is a mind reader, which I doubt."

Mac chuckled softly. "You're the only mind reader I know, Hildy."

"Yes, and don't you forget it."

"There's a bit of a problem. Things aren't as simple as they seem."

"Humph," she exclaimed, nodding her head. "Never are. Especially when matters of the heart are concerned. Now, are you going to tell me what the problem is, or are we going to sit here pussyfooting around being polite all afternoon?"

"You know all the problems we've been having down at the casino?"

Hildy frowned for a moment, wondering what Mac's casino problems had to do with Miss Addy. She nodded suddenly. "You talking about that scoundrel who's been stealing your money?"

Mac nodded. "Remember I told you I brought in someone special to look into the problem? Someone I was sure would be able to find out who and what has been going on?"

"Yes," Hildy said cautiously, wondering where Mac was leading.

"Well, that someone is Addy's grandfather." Although he was supposed to keep Blackie's confidence, Hildy was exempt from secrets. He could and did tell her everything.

Hildy's frown deepened. "I don't understand, Mac. Is this the same grandfather Miss Addy is here looking for?"

"One and the same." Mac sighed heavily. "You see, Hildy, Addy doesn't know about her grandfather's . . .

considerable talents. She thinks he's just a retired gentleman living on a small pension. Addy doesn't have a clue that at one time her grandfather and my grandfather were the best con men in the business."

"Don't you go bad-mouthing your grandpappy, now," Hildy warned. "He may have had his faults, but a finer man you'd never find." Her eyes misted over, and Mac patted her hand in comfort. She had worked for his grandfather for over thirty years. Mac had always suspected Hildy had been in love with his grandfather. It was sad in a way because he had always had the feeling his grandfather was in love with Hildy. But apparently neither had had the courage to tell each other how they felt. What a shame, he thought, determined not to let the same thing happen to him. Love was too rare to let it slip through your fingers.

"You know how I felt about Grandpa," Mac said softly. "But Addy's grandfather is probably the only person other than Grandpa capable of solving *this* problem for me. But he doesn't want Addy to know about his past, or about what he's doing for me."

Hildy's frown deepened until her forehead was creased with wrinkles. "Let me see if I'm following this. Her grandfather's the one you've brought in to solve your little problem, right?"

Mac nodded, taking a sip of his coffee.

"But Addy doesn't know it?"

"Right again," Mac confirmed. "I promised Blackie that I wouldn't tell anyone what he was doing, or even that he was back in town. That was our deal, and the only way I could get him to agree to come out of retirement. I can't go back on my word, Hildy. You know that." Mac dragged a hand through his hair. "But I didn't know about Addy when I made that promise. You see, I hadn't counted on her showing up here. Neither did Blackie. She just presented herself in my office demanding I help her find her grandfather.''

"And?''

"And I told her I would." Mac's lips thinned. "And I intended to, until I realized just *who* her grandfather was.''

"And?'' Hildy prompted again, trying to follow Mac's convoluted story.

Mac sighed heavily. "And then I told her I couldn't help her.''

"Because of your promise to her grandfather?'' This was beginning to make sense, Hildy decided, but just barely.

Mac nodded. "Yes, then when I talked to Blackie and told him Addy was here, looking for him, he made me promise to try and keep her away from the casino, and away from *him* until he finished the job. He reminded me of our agreement, Hildy. What choice did I have? I had to honor my word.''

Hildy shook her head. "Must be getting old, son. I thought Miss Addy told me *you promised to help her* find her grandpa?''

Mac's lips thinned in displeasure. "I did.''

Hildy's head slowly came up. "Wait a minute, I think I'm getting the picture now. That poor child thinks you're going to help her *find* her grandfather, when in fact what you're doing is *keeping* her from finding him?''

"You got it," Mac said glumly, wondering why Hildy seemed to be taking this calmly. She was a woman of principle, and he knew exactly what her reaction to his deception would be. Or at least he had thought he had known. Now, he wasn't so sure.

"So what you're telling me is that you're lying and deceiving Addy?'' Hildy said calmly, much too calmly. Mac should have recognized the ominous tone of her voice. He nodded dismally, feeling a rush of remorse.

Whipping a wooden spoon from the pocket of her apron, Hildy rapped it down hard, barely missing Mac's fingers as he snatched his hand off the table. "MacArthur Cole, I'm ashamed of you! You know better than that. That poor child is genuinely concerned about her kin, and you've got no call to be lying to her. It's not like you, MacArthur." She shook her spoon at him, missing his nose by inches. "I never thought I'd see the day when I'd say I was ashamed of you, boy. But I am." Hildy grabbed her mug of coffee and stood up, but Mac reached out and stopped her.

"Wait, Hildy. There's more."

"I don't know if I want to be hearing any more," she huffed, dropping down heavily into her chair. "But I may as well listen, since you look like you're determined to tell me anyway."

"At first I agreed to keep Addy occupied so her grandfather could go about his business, just like we planned."

"And now?" Hildy looked at him thoughtfully.

"Now, it's much more than that." He dared a glance at her and was relieved to see she was no longer scowling. "I really care about her, Hildy. She's different from any other woman I've ever met. From the moment I laid eyes on her I knew—I just knew—she was something special. Now I want to spend more time with her, not to keep her occupied, but so I can get to know her better. I've never felt this way about a woman before. It was so sudden, and unexpected," Mac added glumly. "I know we haven't known each other that long, but I just feel like it's right."

Hildy laid a hand over Mac's. "Listen, MacArthur, when I met my Harry, I knew the first time I laid eyes on him that he was the one for me. We courted only about a week before we were married. In those days, it just wasn't done. Our families just about disowned us." She chuckled softly. "We were the scandal of the county, we were. People thought I was in a family way because we up and got hitched so fast."

She looked at him sadly. "But, as you know, the Lord didn't bless us with any young'uns. We'd been married only ten years when the Good Lord took him, but they were good years, son. And I learned long ago that time doesn't mean anything when love is concerned. Only felt that way about a man once more in my life, but I was an old bird by then, and well..." Her voice trailed off and Mac couldn't help but wonder if she was thinking about his grandfather. "I'm sorry now I never did anything about it the second time. Love...it's so precious, you've got to grab each moment and savor it."

"There's more," Mac added, causing Hildy to groan softly.

"Now you're not going to tell me Addy's already married, are you? Because if you are, I'm going to get my wooden spoon out again, and this time I won't miss!"

Mac chuckled softly and shook his head. "No, she's not married—yet."

"Yet?" Hildy's gray brows drew into a deep frown. "What does that 'yet' mean?"

"Well, Addy's supposed to be thinking over a proposal from some guy back home. See, she and her grandfather need some money to pay their property taxes. That was the reason her grandfather agreed to come out of retirement. With the money he'll make on this job he's doing for me, he'll have enough to pay the taxes and have plenty left over."

"But Addy doesn't know that?"

Mac shook his head. "No, and I certainly can't tell her. Anyway, this guy back in Muncie offered to give them the money they needed if Addy would marry him."

Hildy drew back looking shocked. "You mean he's buying himself a bride?" She scratched the back of her head, clearly perplexed. "Lordy, Lordy, MacArthur, I thought buying yourself a bride had been outlawed years ago."

Mac's eyes darkened and Hildy realized she'd hit a sore spot. "MacArthur," she said softly. "Does Addy love this fellow?"

"I don't know," Mac answered honestly, realizing he really didn't know if Addy loved Parsnips.

"Well, you best better find out, boy, and soon. There's not much you can do about it if she does. Now, if she doesn't, you're going to have yourself another whole set of problems."

Mac drained his coffee cup, then set it down on the table. "I know. I know."

"Like how you're going to explain to her that while you were supposed to be helping her, you were really hurting her. That's not very nice, MacArthur. But I guess the way you explained it, if her grandpappy doesn't want her to know what he's doing for you, or why, that's his business. You've got no right to interfere with kin. But when all of this comes out in the wash, as surely it will, I just hope Addy's a forgiving soul, because if she's not, you're going to have yourself a heap of problems, and, son, this is one mess I don't have any answers for." Hildy let the words hang in the air, knowing it would cause Mac to do some deep thinking. She picked up their mugs and carried them to the sink as Mac pushed himself away from the table and walked into the living room.

He sank into a leather recliner, trying to put some order to his thoughts. What Hildy said made a lot of sense. He felt terribly guilty about deceiving Addy, particularly with his growing feelings for her. But he knew it couldn't be helped. He'd given his word to Blackie, and he couldn't go back on it now. It wasn't just finding the con man anymore. He now had to consider Blackie's relationship with Addy. He would never do anything to damage that relationship, especially after what Blackie had told him about Addy's mother.

It was a mess, he realized, and for once in his life Mac realized there was no easy answer. He'd just have to take things one at a time. But like Hildy said, he sure hoped Addy had a forgiving nature, because if she didn't . . . he didn't know what he would do.

Addy. Mac smiled. He hadn't felt this way about a woman—ever. And since he'd taken over the casino, he'd been exposed to all sorts of women, each one more beautiful and glamorous than the next. But over the years, Mac realized that outer beauty had nothing to do with what a person was like on the inside. It hadn't taken him long to learn that inner beauty was a rare commodity in this town. From the moment he laid eyes on Addy, he knew she was a woman filled with a deep, inner beauty.

The thought of her spending her life with another man was eating away at him. Why on earth would an attractive woman like Addy want to sell herself short by marrying a man in order to help her out of a jam? He just didn't understand it; there had to be a reason, but what, he didn't know. It just didn't seem logical.

Hildy was right. He had to find out how Addy felt about this guy, and soon. But more importantly, why would Addy want to settle for a marriage of companionship? Mac had a lot of questions and not many answers. The sharp shrill of the telephone jerked him out of his thoughts, and Mac snatched up the receiver before it could wake Addy.

"Hello?"

He was greeted by Blackie's unmistakable chuckle. "That was some fancy footwork in the casino this afternoon, Mac. I've got to admit I was right proud of you."

"You were there?" Mac asked incredulously, wondering how Blackie had managed to see everything without being detected.

"Course I was, son. Probably closer than you think," Blackie added with a mysterious laugh. "I've got to admit

I was a little worried about Addy when those two guards grabbed her. Thought I was going to have to create a little diversion to break her loose, but you came to the rescue in just the nick of time."

Mac was still trying to figure out how Blackie could have witnessed the entire scene without detection. "Where were you?" he inquired, his curiosity eating away at him.

Blackie chuckled again. "I'll never tell. Just remember, you never know where or when I'll show up. Now tell me, where's Addy?"

"Asleep in Rosie's room."

"How on earth did you convince her to stay in the same house with you?" Blackie asked. He knew his granddaughter and her pristine values. He couldn't imagine her consenting to live under the same roof with a man she wasn't married to. His respect for Mac grew. Maybe the kid had some of his grandfather in him after all.

Mac chuckled, adjusting his feet atop the coffee table. "I told her all the rooms in town were booked because of the fight. It was either my house or the park bench."

"And she bought that, did she?" Blackie inquired, quite amused. "You're a devil, MacArthur," Blackie teased as an idea slowly formed in his mind. He liked Mac—a lot. Mac was exactly the kind of man he had hoped Addy would find one day. But she'd never had the chance. Unless he did something, and soon, she was going to spend the rest of her life with that bull-faced drippy-nosed Pernall. Blackie shuddered at the thought. No, sir, he wasn't about to let his beloved granddaughter end up with that bushwhacker. No, sirree, not his Addy. And he was going to do whatever he had to to make sure she didn't. And MacArthur Cole just might figure in with his plans.

"She bought it," Mac confirmed, failing to add that it was the truth. There really were no rooms available in town. He was thoughtful for a moment, wondering how to phrase his next question. "Blackie, tell me something. How does Addy feel about that Parsnips fellow?"

Blackie smiled slyly. Yes, sirree, this was getting more and more interesting by the moment. What he was hearing sounded mighty promising. If Mac was anything like his grandfather—and Blackie had a feeling he was—Mac would not hesitate to go after what he wanted. And he had a feeling MacArthur had already made up his mind about what he wanted. Blackie couldn't have been more pleased.

Surely the kids wouldn't mind if he interfered a bit, kind of helped them along. It would do his heart good. He hadn't had so much fun since he and Frankie worked their last caper, and that was years ago. He took his time answering, waiting to see if Mac squirmed. He did.

"Blackie?" Mac said rather impatiently. "Did you hear me?"

"I heard you," he confirmed. "I may be on in years, but I ain't deaf, son. I was just thinking about it. To tell you the truth, Mac, I'm not rightly sure. I think what she feels for him is more gratitude than anything else. Personally, I've always felt the only reason she kept him around was because it was what her mother would have wanted. Now, for my money, he's not worth the powder to blow him to—"

"Seems to me gratitude is hardly a reason to marry someone," Mac grumbled, causing Blackie to smile again.

"Couldn't agree with you more, my boy. Couldn't agree more. Which is all the more reason that you keep our little secret. If she doesn't have to accept Parsnips's money for the taxes, then maybe she won't feel compelled to marry him."

"Speaking of money, how are things going?" Blackie had been in town almost forty-eight hours and still hadn't given him any clue or indication as to what he had learned.

"I'm making progress, Mac. In fact, I want you to make arrangements for me to have a look at the personnel files tomorrow."

A shudder of apprehension rolled down Mac's spine. He hoped Blackie didn't suspect any of the Parkland's employees. That was an additional problem he sure didn't need right now. "Why the personnel files?"

"I won't know why until I see them now will I? And listen, tonight I've got a date with someone downtown, so if you want to take Addy to dinner, and maybe a show, that might ease her mind a bit. I imagine she's kind of worried about me."

"She is, Blackie," Mac said. "Very worried."

"Well, I've got faith in you, my boy, I'm sure you'll be able to keep her distracted, at least for a few more days."

A few more days. That must mean Blackie was pretty close to cracking this thing, Mac thought glumly. It also meant that Addy would be going back home to Muncie—and Parsnips. The thought brought on a sense of panic. He was going to have to work fast if he was going to convince Addy that there was more to life than Parsnips and Muncie.

"Mac, are you still there?" Blackie asked impatiently.

"I'm here."

"Yes, I think dinner and a show might be just what Addy needs to take her mind off her problems. You know, she's never seen one of those fancy highfalutin' casino shows with the dancing girls and all. I think she might enjoy it." There was a sudden commotion in the background and Blackie suddenly began to whisper. "Listen, son, I've got to run now. I'll check in with you later. Oh, and don't forget, I need to get into the personnel files tomorrow."

The phone went dead in Mac's hands, and he absently dropped it back down into the cradle. *A few more days.* It wasn't much time, but like Hildy said, time didn't matter when the heart was concerned. He just hoped he could make the time count, not only for his sake, but for Addy's, as well.

Chapter Five

Mac!'' Addy said in exasperation, holding on to his arm
to slow him down. "This is ridiculous. I told you back at the
house, I don't have time to be sightseeing or going to shows.
I've got to find my grandfather.''

Ignoring her protests, Mac continued through the Parkland's crowded lobby. "And I told you back at the house,
I'm already working on it. I've contacted the security department, and they've put some men on it. Even though
Rosie's not here, the staff does operate pretty efficiently
without her.''

"Efficient,'' she murmured, quirking one eyebrow. "Are
these the same efficient fellows who took me for a...a...lady
of the evening this morning?'' She flushed and Mac chuckled.

"The same. But I assure you, Addy, they were only doing
their jobs. Their prompt action should inspire confidence.
If your grandfather's in this casino tonight, I guarantee security will find him.'' Mac deliberately phrased his words so

there would be no more lies between them. He didn't want to add to the list of things he had deceived her about. Had Blackie *been* in the casino this evening, security *would* have found him. But Mac knew Blackie was nowhere near the Parkland, so at least that part of his statement had been truthful. "Addy, please, will you try to relax?"

"Relax," she muttered, allowing him to lead her across the crowded casino. "I'm not even dressed for this," she complained, glancing at the elegantly clad women waiting in line to see the dinner show. Addy felt self-conscious in her plain skirt and white blouse. She didn't own any elegant clothes, at least nothing that would be suitable for this type of evening. She'd never had the need for anything extravagant. Blouses and skirts were fine for daytime and for her weekly date with Pernall.

"It's Hildy's bridge night, Addy. We had to go out to eat anyway, so what's the harm in taking in a show while we're having dinner? That is, unless you have some objection to doing two things at once?" he teased. He bent and kissed the tip of her nose, wanting to erase the worry lines from her face. "And you look beautiful," he insisted, coming to a halt and pinning her with his gaze. "You'd look beautiful no matter what you wore." The expression on his face sent a thrill through her, and she reached up and touched his face.

"Thank you," she whispered. When Mac looked at her like that, she *felt* beautiful.

"Come on, now. Stick close to me." Tucking her arm into his, Mac led them into the theater.

An elegant waiter dressed in a black tuxedo ushered them to a plush velvet booth in the VIP section. The room was huge. The long tables nearest the stage accommodated up to fourteen people, and the middle of the room was ringed with booths. The seating was a leveled tier, so that no matter where you sat you had a good view of the enormous stage and all the action.

It was nearly an hour until show time. Addy could hear the hustle and bustle going on backstage in preparation for the performance, and in spite of her misgivings, her excitement began to grow. Although she had been to the movies many times, she'd never actually seen a live performance, particularly one of this magnitude, if the brochure the maître d' had handed her was to be believed.

The lobster they ordered was delicious, and all through dinner Mac regaled her with stories about Rosie and the casino business. They laughed and talked, and Addy found herself relaxing. Mac made it easy for her to drop her guard. Perhaps it was because he made her feel comfortable, so much so that she found she wasn't quite so anxious about her grandfather. Knowing Mac had people working on locating him also eased her fears—somewhat. Mac had asked her to trust him, and Addy found she did—implicitly. He had done nothing but try to help her. As they sat and chatted over coffee before the show began, Addy found that Mac really listened to what she had to say; he seemed genuinely interested in her opinions.

Addy couldn't help thinking that for such an ominous looking character, MacArthur Cole had a long, strong streak of sweetness in him.

"Are you having a good time?" Mac asked, covering Addy's hand with his. She turned to him and smiled. "I'm having a wonderful time." The lights in the theater dimmed.

"Oh, Mac," Addy breathed, squeezing his hand as the show started, "everything is simply incredible." The orchestra began its opening strains and a bevy of beautiful girls dressed in glorious costumes high kicked their way across the elaborately decorated stage to thunderous applause. Addy sat forward in anticipation.

Mac smiled at her enthusiasm. He had seen the show thousands of times, but had never quite appreciated all the grandeur and splendor until he had seen it tonight through Addy's eyes. She had a special way of looking at things, a way that made everything seem fresh and new to him.

"I'm glad you're enjoying it," he whispered, leaning close until the scent of him infiltrated her breathing space, making her feel warm and giddy. She glanced down self-consciously, vividly aware that just his touch made her heart pound wickedly. Mac radiated a warm vitality that made her feel so alive.

He was having quite an effect on her, an effect that she was powerless to resist. Being with Mac was addictive and intoxicating. She glanced at him shyly. He had changed into a sleek pin-striped gray suit, a conservative starched white shirt and a blue-and-red silk tie. His dark hair looked squeaky clean and still fell with reckless abandon, giving him somewhat of a boyish look. He was so handsome he almost took her breath away.

Turning her attention toward the stage, Addy decided she had to stop thinking about Mac if only for her own peace of mind and heart. She had to stop letting her imagination run away with her. But it was hard with Mac sitting right next to her. So near, she thought sadly, and yet so very far.

Directing her attention toward the stage, Addy was soon totally entranced by the high-spirited show. She watched as the beautiful girls paraded proudly across the stage, their long shapely legs waving in the air, their faces gleaming under the shimmering lights.

Most of the show girls were tall, with manes of glorious hair that fell seductively to their waists. Their costumes were bright canary, decorated with sequins and beads that sparkled under the stage lights. On their heads they wore enormous headpieces of matching yellow ostrich feathers, making Addy wonder how on earth they managed to keep their balance.

Addy watched in wide-eyed fascination. She had never seen anything quite so spectacular. The stage, the costumes, the elaborate dance numbers, it was all mesmerizing.

Addy tried not to be envious, but it was hard. The women on the stage were so beautiful, so glamorous. Oh, just once to be adorned with sequins and feathers, to be beautiful and . . . adored. Oh, just once to be able to do something so wonderful, so exciting the memories would remain forever.

Shouldn't a woman have at least one reckless memory to hang on to? Addy wondered wistfully. Just *once* shouldn't she be able to have some treasured, precious memory tucked away in the corners of her mind, something she could go back and reminisce about as the years unfolded?

It's a sin to want more when others have so much less. You have to learn to appreciate what you have.

Her mother's words reverberated in her mind, and Addy gave a heavy sigh. Why was it so wrong for her to just once wish for something she'd never had?

"Addy, is something wrong?" Mac touched her shoulder and she blinked away the painful memories.

"Wh . . . what?"

Mac cocked his head and looked at her thoughtfully, disturbed by the sudden shadow in her beautiful green eyes. "The show's almost over and you're frowning, what's wrong?" He moved closer, genuinely concerned. "Didn't you like the performance?"

Addy took a deep breath, trying to calm herself. This was ridiculous. What on earth was happening to her? She should be sitting here appreciating the show instead of feeling sorry for herself! How ungrateful she must seem.

"Oh, Mac, no," she breathed. "I loved the show." She smiled shyly. "This was the most beautiful thing I've ever seen. I'm so glad we came."

Mac cocked his head and looked at her. Despite her protests, he had a feeling something was disturbing her. His fingers gently brushed against the back of her neck, and Addy shivered as he moved closer. Her breathing slowed, and her heart seemed to pound so loudly she was afraid Mac might hear it.

"Addy," he said softly, looking deep into her troubled eyes. He saw no coyness, no deception, just honesty and goodness and a faint shadow of sadness that even her smile couldn't hide. Something tugged at his heart. The thought that something was hurting Addy hurt him. "What is it? Something's bothering you, Addy. Why don't you tell me?" he coaxed. "Is it your grandfather?" he asked guiltily.

"No," she admitted truthfully. Because of Mac she was no longer worried about her grandfather. What she was worried about were her growing feelings for the man sitting next to her.

How had things gotten so out of control so quickly? she wondered. Less than forty-eight hours ago she had been back home in Muncie, safe and secure in her normal, boring life.

Now, in just a few hours, because of one man, her safe, boring, normal life had been turned upside down. She had always thought Pernall and Muncie would be enough for her. Now Addy wasn't so sure. The thought brought on a mixture of fear and guilt, feelings she wasn't quite sure she could handle, not with her complicated feelings toward Mac.

In the past twenty-four hours, she'd experienced more of life than she had in the past twenty-three years. Feelings and emotions she'd never dreamed possible were now locked in her memory. Memories she knew she would treasure forever.

She had no idea how it was possible to feel so close to, or so comfortable with Mac when she hadn't known anyone like him in her whole life. But she did.

Shyly her gaze met his. He seemed genuinely interested in what was disturbing her. She could tell by the sincerity in his eyes, the tenderness of his voice. Although Pernall was a dear man, she had a difficult time opening up to him. Perhaps it was because she always felt as if he wasn't quite paying attention, or perhaps it was the fact that she wasn't quite convinced he was really interested in what she had to say.

"Addy?" Mac prompted, sliding his arm around her and clearly not willing to let the matter drop. His fingers gently coaxed and comforted her, caressing the back of her neck.

She could feel his touch all the way down to her toes. Suddenly Addy felt the warmth of him, the kindness of him and something else.

His eyes darkened as they narrowed on her mouth. The urge to kiss her was nearly overwhelming, but Mac controlled himself—with effort. "Addy?" Mac whispered. "Please tell me, what's wrong?" The silent plea in his voice was so tender, so concerned, Addy felt her heart constrict.

He wound his fingers through her hair, drawing her closer, and her eyes widened. *God, how he wanted to kiss her.* Not now, he cautioned himself.

"Please," he said softly, his gaze holding hers. "It's important to me." He suddenly wanted to know everything about Addy. *Everything.*

She nodded, unable to look Mac in the eyes. She'd never discussed this—her innermost thoughts and feelings with anyone...ever. Perhaps it was because there had never been anyone to discuss them with.

Addy swallowed hard, suddenly sorry about the things in life she couldn't change.

For some reason, tonight, more than ever before, she felt a pang of regret for all the things she had never done, for all the opportunities she had missed, all the things she'd never seen or never had a chance to experience. Perhaps it was because tonight, for the first time, she *was* experiencing all of the things she never had the opportunity to explore before.

It had never really bothered her that she had missed so much, at least not until today. They say you can't miss something you've never had, but sadly Addy realized that wasn't true.

Stop this! she chided herself. She should have been appreciating the evening and not lamenting about what she had missed.

"Come on, Addy," Mac coaxed, drawing her into the comfort of his arms until she felt the gentle pounding of his heart next to hers. "Don't you know some things are easier to handle if you share the burden?"

She glanced at Mac, sorely tempted to brush the whole thing off, but the look in his eyes stopped her. For some reason, she had a feeling Mac would understand.

Slowly, tentatively she began, no longer feeling foolish. "Watching the show tonight, seeing all those beautiful girls, I don't know..." Addy smiled wanly, trying to lessen the importance of what she was about to say. She didn't think she could bear it if Mac laughed at her or ridiculed her. "I guess I was just thinking about how beautiful those girls were. It must be wonderful," she finished lamely, suddenly feeling acutely embarrassed.

"Addy," Mac said gently, realizing this was obviously something very important to her. "Don't you know how beautiful *you* are?"

"Me?" Her eyes widened in shock. She tried to laugh, but it didn't quite come out right, and Mac felt something tug deeply at his heart. She shook her head. "Mac, I know what I look like. You don't need to flatter me, it doesn't bother me, really." She tried to smile again. "There are other things in life besides beauty."

One dark brow lifted and Mac cocked his head. "Addy, I agree with you, there are other things in life. But where on earth did you ever get the idea you weren't beautiful?" She suddenly averted her gaze, and once again Mac had a feeling he'd hit a nerve, a particularly sensitive one. He decided to try another approach. "Addy, look at me. *Look at me,*" he commanded, turning her chin toward him so she had no choice. "What do you see?"

Addy stared at Mac's beautiful eyes and handsome face. She took a deep breath. "I see a very handsome, very kind man," she said quietly, unable to drag her gaze from his.

"Don't you see this?" he asked, taking her hand and placing it gently on the jagged scar that ran the length of his face. Addy stared at him. Funny, when she looked at Mac, she didn't see his scar, well, certainly not the way he meant. It was there, but it wasn't important. It was just part of him. When she looked at Mac, all she saw was a wonderful, kind, attractive man.

"Not really," she admitted, gently caressing the angry red mark. She'd never touched a man so freely or so intimately before. But with Mac, she wasn't the least bit self-conscious. "How did . . ." Her voice trailed off. Maybe this was something Mac didn't care to discuss. Besides, it really wasn't any of her business.

"How did I get the scar?" Mac smiled grimly. "Compliments of my stepfather."

"Oh, Mac," Addy gasped. Her hand flew to her mouth. "I'm so sorry." A few silent moments passed. The theater was dark now, the stage silent. The room was empty except for Addy and Mac and a few busboys cleaning up.

"Don't be sorry, honey," Mac finally said quietly, "it was a long time ago." She could feel the tension tighten his body. His jaw clenched for a moment. "After my father died, my mother had a rough time of it. She wasn't on very good terms with my grandfather, and financially, times were rough. Scott was a successful businessman, and my mother thought we'd have security if she married him. What she didn't realize was that he had a ferocious temper. My sister, Rosie, and I were his favorite targets. One day he started in on my sister for something. Rosie is small like you and couldn't really defend herself, so I stepped in to stop him. I was only about sixteen, but I was big for my age. I pulled him off my sister, and the next thing I knew he picked up a bottle and smashed it across my face." Mac absently fingered the scar with his free hand, his eyes growing dark. "That was the last time he ever raised a hand to either one of us." He was quiet for a long moment, and Addy reached out and touched his hand, aching for him. Everyone had their own private pain, she thought, feeling a rush of warmth for Mac.

"I packed up everything Rosie and I had and left. That's when we went to live with Hildy. She had been my grandfather's housekeeper for as long as I could remember. We had no place else to go. And even though my grandfather was gone, Hildy took us in, no questions asked. She's been with us ever since." He paused for a moment, deep in thought.

"You see, hon," he began slowly. "I know the scar is there, it's been there every single day for the past fourteen years. A reminder of what can happen when a woman marries for security instead of love."

Addy flushed, knowing he was referring to her possible marriage to Pernall and the conversation they'd had earlier in his office. Now she understood what he meant about gambling with marriage. No wonder Mac felt if she married Pernall it would be a bigger gamble than her grandfather was taking by gambling for the tax money. Addy pushed the disturbing thought aside.

Pernall would never strike her, of that she was sure. But what else did she really know about him? Oh, she'd known him her whole life; they'd grown up together. But what did she really know about him? She'd never really thought about it before. She had spent more time talking with Mac about things in just one evening than she had in many years with Pernall.

Tonight, right now, she knew more about Mac, felt closer to him, than she'd ever felt toward Pernall.

"Addy?" Mac covered her hand with his, gently rubbing his thumb across her tender skin, sending goose bumps winging up her arms. "Now, what about you? Who told you that you weren't beautiful?"

Addy stiffened. This was something she had never, never discussed with anyone. It was too personal, too embarrassing. She had never admitted to anyone—not even her grandfather—what a disappointment she had been to her mother. It wasn't something she was particularly proud of, what daughter would be? It was a secret shame Addy had endured silently.

She had guarded her painful secret for so many years she wasn't even sure she could talk about it. It was a hurt that had scarred her deeply, one she had lived with for as long as she could remember. To talk about it now, to bring it out in the open, particularly with Mac, was something she wasn't certain she could do.

Mac drew her closer, pressing her head down to the comfort of his shoulder. She hadn't uttered a single word, yet Mac knew whatever it was was very painful to her. The thought caused his heart to ache.

"It's all right," he soothed, stroking the back of her silky head. "Some things just take time to talk about. But I'm here, Addy, and when you feel up to talking, you just go right ahead. I'll wait."

She turned her face toward his shoulder, allowing herself to lean into Mac, weariness suddenly overtaking her. Her throat constricted and she blinked back tears. It had been so very long since anyone had held her or offered her comfort.

Memories reached out and assaulted Addy, memories she thought long buried, but now they rose up to haunt her, engulfing her in a deep sadness.

Other than her grandfather, she couldn't remember the last time someone had hugged her. Certainly not her mother.

As a child, her mother had paid little attention to her, except to admonish or scold her, or to remind her she was no great beauty. Perhaps if her mother hadn't been so beautiful it wouldn't have mattered so much, but she was, and it did.

She fought back tears as they sat silently. Addy allowed herself to be wrapped in the cocoon of Mac's arms. Was it time to share her memories? Would sharing them take some of the pain away?

Addy grew very still, took a deep breath and began slowly. "My mother was a very beautiful woman. I never really knew much about her childhood, because she refused to talk about it except to say her father—Blackie—was a shiftless vagabond. She didn't have very much respect for him. In fact, when I was little, she was always telling me I was just like him." Her voice, low and pain filled, cracked a bit.

"The Simpsons were one of Muncie's leading families," Addy went on quietly. "When my mother married my father, she broke off all ties with her own family. My father's family had lived in Muncie for generations, and my mother was determined to fit in with them.'' Her tentative smile faltered then slowly faded. Mac's fingers tightened on her shoulder for a moment, reminding her he was there.

"When I was born, she was determined that I, too, fit in with the Simpsons. But I just never did. I wasn't blessed with my mother's natural beauty, a fact she constantly reminded me of. I was a big disappointment to her because I wasn't the daughter she wanted or expected.''

Mac's eyes briefly slid closed. Dear God. His chest hurt from his exploding emotions. He wanted to strike out at someone—anyone—who had hurt Addy.

"I guess I resembled my grandfather's side of the family, and that always annoyed my mother. She wanted no reminders of her own family, people she was ashamed of, and I guess I fit right into that mold—a constant, daily reminder.'' Addy's voice grew thin and brittle as each word seemed to rip away a small piece inside of her. "To this day, Mac, I have no idea why she despised her father so. I've never understood it. If you knew Grandpa, you'd understand what I mean.''

"Addy.'' His words came out a husky whisper. He couldn't stand this deception any longer. He didn't ever want to cause Addy another moment of pain. He was going to tell her the truth and let the consequences be damned. "Addy, please, listen—''

She raised her hand to stop him. She'd started now and she wanted to finish, fearing if she didn't, she might never find the courage again.

"After my father died, my mother was more determined than ever that I live up to the Simpson name and place in society. But I just never seemed to be able to do the things she wanted. Oh, I tried, Mac, I really tried. But I just wasn't interested in tea parties or the opera. I thought it was stuffy and boring. I wanted to travel the world, to see things and do things." Addy paused and Mac tightened his arms around her. He could hear the anguish buried deep within as she continued. "I wanted to paint and write." Her face grew animated for a moment. "I wanted to travel the country, making my own way, painting the landscape and writing about my experiences." She grew still and silent, suddenly glancing away.

"One day my mother and I had a terrible fight. I was young and impulsive, I guess, and I was sick and tired of always trying to live up to her expectations of excellence and always failing." Addy stopped, unable to go on. Mac nodded in sympathy, holding her gently. "During our fight, I told her that as soon as I was old enough I was going to leave Muncie, and the Simpson legacy, and never come back. I wanted to see what life had to offer besides Muncie. Naturally, she was appalled.

"Mother kept saying she didn't understand why she had been cursed with such an ungrateful child who was certainly going to be the death of her." The breath left Mac on an urgent hiss, but he refused to comment until she finished. There would be time enough to talk. Now, it was Addy's turn to let it all out.

"My... mother accused me of being just like my grandfather, someone she despised. I knew then exactly how she felt about me. She told me that I was a selfish brat who didn't appreciate what I had and was always wanting more. She told me it was a sin to want more when others had so much less." Her voice had softened until he almost had to strain to hear her. He stroked her hair, his hands gentle and soothing, trying to erase the ache she had carried for so many years.

"My mother was furious, livid, in fact. She told me that I'd better appreciate what I had, because there would be little else for me anywhere. She said it was time I accepted the fact that I was no great beauty, and no man would ever come calling for my looks. My only hope was to develop my mind, because that was—" Addy's voice broke "—the only way a man would ever want me."

She heard Mac's quick intake of breath and felt his arms tighten around her as he rocked her gently to and fro. She lifted a hand and clung to the front of his shirt, allowing herself to lean on him to accept the comfort she had been denied for so very long as the tears finally came. Tears she had not allowed herself to let go of for so many years.

She'd thought the pain had dimmed with the memory; she'd thought the years would take away the sting. But it hadn't, and it shocked her. She couldn't remember the last time she had ever allowed herself to lose control like this.

Mac felt a sudden and deep contempt for the woman who had called herself Addy's mother. How could she do it? he wondered, his heart aching for Addy. He wanted to stop the pain that terrorized Addy and was now terrorizing him. After a few tension-filled moments, Addy lifted her head and continued, not bothering to hide or wipe away the tears that slid quietly down her cheeks.

"The day after our fight my mother was so upset with me she refused to speak to me, let alone look at me. She just kept telling me I was an ugly, ungrateful child. She kept asking what she had ever done to be cursed with me." Addy suddenly tensed. "That evening she had a fatal heart attack," Addy whispered softly, wiping a tear from her cheek. "Oh, Mac, it was all my fault. If I hadn't been such a disappointment to her, if only I could have been the kind of daughter she wanted and deserved." Deep racking sobs broke loose, and Addy buried her head on Mac's waiting shoulder.

How could it still hurt after all these years? How could she still ache after so long?

Mac's arms tightened around her until she could feel the warmth of his body and the beating of his own heart against hers. Silently she let the tears come. Mac held her close, letting her cry until there were no more tears.

Drained and exhausted, Addy took a deep, shuddering breath and wearily leaned closer to Mac, grateful for the warmth of his arms. Her eyes fluttered closed as a peacefulness she'd never known slowly swept over her.

How many days and nights had she wished for someone to hold her, to comfort her, to make her feel she was worth something? How many nights had she cried herself to sleep, blaming herself for things she couldn't change?

She'd been lonely for so long. Until tonight, she'd never realized just how lonely she'd been—until she'd met Mac. To hear another heart beating so close to hers, to feel the warmth of another human being holding her, comforting her, was a soothing balm for all the pain she'd endured silently, privately for so long.

Trying to calm the fire in her lungs, Addy took several deep breaths. Her body felt spent, drained, and she'd been leaning against Mac for so long that she feared his shoulder might have frozen.

She sat up and wiped her eyes with the back of her hand. "I'm sorry," she said quietly, unable to meet his gaze.

"Don't be." He knew there was more; he didn't want to push her, but he wanted to hear it all. "What happened after she died, Addy?"

She shrugged and looked off into the distance of the dark theater. "After my mother's death, I realized she had been right. I had been selfish and ungrateful. I should have appreciated all that I had, and not always yearned for more."

Her words caused Mac's heart to constrict. *No, Addy,* he thought. *Your mother was wrong, oh, so wrong.* Everything seemed to still inside of Mac as Addy looked up at him. Her green eyes were wide and soulful, bleak and yearning. His heart welled with emotion as longing spread like liquid fire through him. What he felt was neither pity nor sympathy, but something else, something much, much more. A yearning to possess Addy, to fill her soul with all the things she had too little of—kindness, compassion, confidence, security, but most importantly, love. Mac knew, just then, he was going to give Addy all of the things she'd missed in life. But more importantly he wanted to share them with her; he wanted to show her how beautiful life could be, how beautiful love could be. He had a feeling she had no idea, but she would.

"Maybe if I'd been a different person, a better person, maybe she'd still be alive. From that day on, I knew I had to try to live up to what my mother had always expected of me. I decided I would stay in Muncie just like she wanted, and try to fit in. I learned to accept myself for what I was—there really was no point in not facing reality. I knew I was no great beauty. So I kept myself neat and clean like she wanted, and I developed my mind. I stayed in Muncie and kept Simpson House in the family because I knew that would have been what she wanted."

Rarely did Mac lose his temper, but at the moment, if he could have gotten his hands on Miss Adeline Simpson's mother, he would have strangled her.

"Grandpa came to Muncie shortly after Mother's death to take care of me. It's funny, my mother was as different from her father as I was from her. I was only twelve, and despite the way my mother had felt about Grandpa, I fell in love with him instantly. When he came, he brought Aunt Myrtle and Walter with him." Addy laughed softly. "If Mother could have seen them, she really would have had a fit. But, in our own way, we were a family. I love all of them, Mac. My grandfather is very, very special. I love him very much." Addy lifted her head and looked at him. Her eyes sparkled with unshed tears. "Now do you understand why I have to find my grandfather, and why I have to save the family home?"

Mac nodded. He understood, but he sure as hell didn't agree with her. "Addy," he said quietly, his voice soft and gentle. "Your mother was wrong."

Her head snapped up and she looked at him. No one had ever said her mother was wrong before. *No one.* Addy was much too practical to ignore the truth. "Mac, please—"

"Let me finish, Addy. Your mother *was* wrong. She judged beauty by what a person looks like on the outside. But beauty has *nothing* to do with a person's appearance. Beauty—real beauty—is what's *inside* of a person. My stepfather was a handsome son of a gun, but he was the ugliest person I've ever met. You see, Addy, if you don't have the beauty *inside*, it doesn't matter what's on the outside. For my money, honey, you can take all of the artificial outer beauty, all the glitz and glamour, and toss it in the nearest trash can, because *if a person isn't beautiful on the inside, what's outside doesn't matter.*" He smiled. "You're lucky, Addy," he whispered, his eyes gently caressing her face. "You're not only beautiful on the outside, but more importantly, you're beautiful on the inside, where it counts."

Addy stared at Mac, overcome. She tried to hold back the tears. "I don't want your pity, Mac," she said stiffly, turning away.

Mac grabbed her shoulders and forced her to look at him. "Pity? Addy, I don't have one ounce of pity for you. You don't need my pity." His eyes gently went over her face, taking in every inch of her. He raised a finger and touched her lips, her cheeks, her brows, pausing to wipe the dampness from her eyes. "You are beautiful, Miss Adeline Simpson, inside and out." He cradled her face in his hands, his eyes warm and sincere. "Beautiful," he repeated softly.

Never had anyone told her she was beautiful—inside or out. *Mac thought she was beautiful.* It was the loveliest thing anyone had ever said to her. Her heart overflowed with joy.

Mac bent and gently brushed his lips across hers. Addy's eyes fluttered closed.

"Oh, Mac," she whispered as a lone tear slipped down her cheek.

"Addy." Mac hauled her body close, trying to absorb all the pain and hurt she had endured. His heart and soul ached for her. Somehow, someway, he had to tell her, to show her, her mother had been wrong. Very, very wrong. Adeline Simpson was one of the most beautiful women he had ever had the pleasure of meeting.

Addy sighed heavily. Her mind knew she couldn't afford to let her growing feelings for Mac interfere with her concern for her grandfather and her purpose for being here. But Addy realized where Mac was concerned, she no longer had the ability to think with her mind, only with her heart.

When she was with Mac, he made her *feel* like the most beautiful person in the world. He made her feel good about herself, a luxury Addy had never been afforded before. Just once, just for one brief shining moment, she wanted to be selfish and savor the moment. Addy nestled closer to Mac, feeling his warmth. She took a deep, shuddering breath, allowing Mac's intoxicating scent to comfort her as she tried to control the flow of tears. Her weeping was soft, silent, and it tore through Mac's heart.

Oh, Addy. Mac held her close, rocking her gently as his heart pounded. Never before had another human being ever touched him the way Addy had.

Addy was different from any woman he had ever met. And Mac had a feeling, a deep gut instinctive feeling, that she was the one woman he'd been waiting for his whole life—the woman he wanted to spend the rest of his life with.

No matter how he tried to deny it, he was falling in love with Miss Adeline Simpson from Muncie, Indiana.

Wonderful, Mac thought grimly. *He was in love with a woman who planned to spend the rest of her life with an-*

other man! As always, when Mac thought of the other man in Addy's life, his insides coiled. A sudden thought occurred to him and he frowned. Things were suddenly beginning to fall into place. Hadn't Blackie said Addy was going to marry Pernall because it's what her mother would have wanted?

"Addy?"

She pulled out of his arms, wiped her eyes with the back of her hand and glanced up at him. She tried to smile, suddenly embarrassed by her behavior. "What, Mac?" She sniffled softly.

"Now, I'd like to ask you a question, and I want you to think about it before you answer." Addy nodded, waiting. "How...how...do you feel about this Pernall fellow?"

Pernall! Addy's heart began to pound in sudden trepidation. Merciful Heaven! She'd completely forgotten about Pernall. Guilt washed over her. When she was with Mac, she thought of nothing but him.

"How do I feel about him?" she repeated, stalling for time.

"Do you love him?" Mac demanded, holding his breath as he waited for her answer.

Addy blinked. "Love?"

"Yes, do you love him?" Mac demanded again.

"I don't know," she answered honestly.

"Then why the hell are you planning to marry him?" Mac asked, totally befuddled. It didn't make sense. Aside from the money issue, what other reason could she have?

"He's very kind," she repeated, realizing she was beginning to sound like a broken record. "And it's what Mother would have wanted. Don't forget," she added softly, "he also offered to give me the money I need to pay the taxes on Simpson House." Her reasons sounded feeble even to her own ears.

His jaw tightened. "I told you in my office, Addy, bargaining your hand in marriage for a few lousy dollars is not a reason to marry someone."

"It's what my mother would have wanted," she repeated again, causing Mac to scowl.

"Addy, if your mother was wrong about your being beautiful, isn't it possible she could be wrong about the man you should marry? How do you know who you want to marry? You've never even been out of Muncie. Addy, there's so much more to life, so much to see and do, so many people to meet, things to experience. You weren't wrong to want those things. It's only natural to want to experience some of life. Your mother was wrong, Addy, about you, your beauty, about life and even about Parsnips."

"No, Mac." Addy shook her head firmly. That kind of selfish thinking had gotten her into trouble before. The burden of her guilt weighed heavily all these years. She had no wish to add to her burden when she could barely carry the one she had now. "Pernall's good and kind, and he'll be a good companion." Why did the thought of spending the rest of her life with Pernall suddenly make her want to cry?

Mac sighed in exasperation. He was right about Addy, she was stubborn. But so was he. He had waited his whole life for her, and he wasn't about to hand her over to some other man who didn't even love her, without one hell of a fight. Fighting for what he wanted came naturally to Mac, but for Addy, he was ready to wage the fight of his life.

"Addy," Mac grumbled. "Those are certainly not reasons to agree to spend your life with someone. Believe me, I know firsthand what a marriage made without love can bring." Absently Mac ran his finger along the length of his scar, and Addy knew he was thinking about his mother. Mac uttered an oath of disgust. "*This is your life we're talking about*. It's not a sin to want more from a marriage than companionship and kindness.'' His gaze pinned hers. ''What about love, Addy?''

Love. She had never really thought about love in connection with marriage. She'd always felt that love was for others. How on earth could she ever expect *anyone* to love her, when her own mother hadn't?

Using his free hand, he tilted her chin up, his blue eyes fixed on hers. ''Addy, marriage is much too important to go into without love. Surely you must realize that. There has to be some other way to save Simpson House. Hell, I'll *give* you the money.'' The moment the words were out, he knew it was the wrong thing to say.

She shook her head firmly. ''I appreciate the offer, Mac, I really do. But I've never taken a handout from anyone, and I certainly couldn't start now.''

A frown rumpled his brow and Mac rubbed his scar thoughtfully. He should have expected that. Mac realized he wasn't handling this very well, but nothing had ever been so important to him before, and nothing mattered right now but making Addy see what she was doing was wrong. He couldn't let her marry Pernall. *He couldn't.* He had to let her know how important she was to him.

''Addy?'' The hand at her chin gently caressed her face, and Addy trembled at the look in his eyes, vividly aware of the sudden tension between them. It was humming in the air, drawing them closer, and Addy felt powerless to stop it. He whispered her name once again, and slowly lowered his face toward hers until nothing but Mac filled her vision.

Oh, Mac. Her heart constricted as anticipation flooded through her, heating her blood.

Oh, Addy. His breath came quickly, his emotions overloading his thoughts. Addy lifted her hands to his chest, and she could feel his heart thudding wildly against his shirt. It matched the rate of her own.

His mouth slowly covered hers, tentatively at first, until she relaxed against him, sliding her hands up the front of his shirt and around his neck.

Mac tasted warm and sweet, much softer than she'd ever expected. His lips moved over hers, claiming, possessive. She felt herself turn pliant, knowing what she was feeling was good and right and *wonderful*.

Mac's eyes fluttered closed as he combed his fingers through her hair, pulling her closer, wanting to taste all of her.

Addy gasped as Mac's mouth gently coaxed a heated response from her. Her pulse thudded as she moved with him, their lips holding, tasting, savoring.

The pressure of his kiss increased as a soft moan of desire escaped her lips. She caressed the dark silky hair at the nape of his neck, marveling at all the different textures of him. The softness of his mouth, the hardness of his chest, the silkiness of his hair, the gentleness of his arms. How was it possible that one kiss, one man, could arouse so many different feelings in her? Addy shivered in the darkened theater.

Instinctively she knew this was the way a woman was supposed to be kissed. This was the way a kiss was supposed to feel. She leaned into Mac, anxious to feel him, to touch him and to have him touch her. She heard a soft moan slip through his lips as he pulled her even closer, until they were pressed chest to chest.

Prudence and caution flew out the window as Addy forgot about the strict rigidity of her upbringing and thought only of what she was feeling. From the moment when their eyes had met in Mac's office, she knew there was something special between them, a spark that had now suddenly ignited into an inferno, engulfing them both.

Mac's breath quickened as his mouth savored Addy's sweetness. Lord, he'd wanted to kiss her since he'd first laid eyes on her. Wanted to hold her in his arms, and not just for a moment—but forever.

Mac slowly drew back, not wanting the kiss to end but knowing it had to. He had to go slow; he didn't want to scare Addy. His heartbeat was irregular, his breathing short and raspy.

"Well, well, well," came a deep drawl from behind, startling them. Addy and Mac jumped apart guiltily. Mac turned, surprised to find Harry, the man Addy had had a run-in with this afternoon. "What have we here?" he asked, looking at them quizzically. "What have we here?"

Mac glanced at Addy, grinning devilishly. "We're kissing cousins," he explained to Harry, reaching for Addy and ignoring the man's stunned expression. Muttering under his breath, Harry walked off shaking his head. Addy and Mac burst into laughter.

"Do you think he believed us?" Mac asked, reaching for her again. Addy's eyes were shining, and she went willingly into his arms.

"I don't know," she whispered, anxious to feed the sudden hunger Mac had aroused.

His mouth covered hers again, this time with more urgency. Addy turned to liquid, winding her arms tightly around him, linking her fingers together in an effort to hold him tight. The moment was so magical, so precious, she didn't want it to end.

This would be her one reckless, cherished memory. The one she could go back to over and over again as the years with Pernall unfolded.

No!

She didn't want this to be all that she had. Addy realized she wanted more. There had to be more to life than one cherished moment, one precious kiss. So much more.

Had her mother been wrong?
Was Mac right?

She suddenly didn't know anymore.

Mac slowly withdrew from her. "Addy?" His eyes lingered on her swollen lips as desire once again rose up to tempt him.

"Yes, Mac?" she whispered, still staring into his beautiful eyes.

"I—I—" A shrill ring split through the air and Addy jumped as the sound echoed in the silent theater. "Damn!" Mac said, reaching down to shut off his beeper. "Addy, I have to get to a phone. Stay here, I'll be right back." She nodded, grateful for a few moments alone to sort out her thoughts. Sliding out of the booth, Mac bent down and grazed his lips across hers possessively, sending a quick hot thrill through her. "I'll be right back."

Addy hugged herself, suddenly cold and confused. She stared into the darkened theater, her thoughts scrambling, swirling in a million different directions. Was Mac right? she wondered again.

Mac. A small smile curved her lips. Never in her wildest dreams had she ever expected to meet anyone like him. He was warm, caring and tender. And, Merciful Heaven, she was falling in love with him!

The thought brought on a round of sadness. Was she crazy? How on earth had she let her emotions slip so far out of control? She was supposed to be searching for her grandfather and thinking over Pernall's proposal—not falling in love with another man!

Oh, Mac, she thought wistfully. He was all the things she had ever dreamed about—silly schoolgirl dreams she had always thought were for someone else, not for her. But now, Addy knew, they weren't just silly dreams. Love could be a reality for her, too—if she had the courage to go after it. Did she? Dare she take a chance? Was it selfish to want something more than Muncie and Pernall?

"Addy?" Mac rushed back, his face flushed. "We have to go home and pack." He reached out and took her hand, tugging her out of the booth.

"Pack?" She stared at him in bewilderment, startled by his announcement. Her heart began to race in fear and she clutched his sleeve. "Grandpa?" Her face grew ashen. "Has something happened to Grandpa?"

Mac drew her into the comfort of his arms. "No, nothing like that. That call was from the head of security at our Reno casino. It seems someone fitting your grandfather's description was seen at the Parkland hotel in Reno this evening." He drew back and looked at her, relieved to see the color coming back into her face. "I thought it might be a good idea for us to go down to Reno to check it out."

The call he had received was actually about a minor problem here at the Vegas Parkland and had absolutely nothing to do with Blackie *or* Reno. But Mac had made a decision. He had only a few days—at best—to prove to Addy that there was more to life than Muncie and Pernall. And he knew very well he was going to have a heck of a time getting her to concentrate on anything but finding her grandfather if they remained in Vegas. The idea of heading for Reno was a brainstorm.

Mac quickly made the arrangements, then left a message for Blackie so he wouldn't become alarmed at their sudden disappearance. He also gave Blackie carte blanche to go anywhere, without question, in the entire Parkland hotel and casino chain, hoping that would pacify him into not questioning why Mac had suddenly taken off with his beloved granddaughter. Mac wanted a few days alone with Addy, a few days to show her—to tell her—that there could be a whole lot more to life, including love.

"But, Mac," she protested. "What about your casino here? You can't just up and take off like that, can you?"

Mac grinned. "That's the best part of being the boss. I can do whatever I want." He dropped a kiss to her forehead. "And what I want right now is to go to Reno, with you. Besides," he added, "don't you remember Hildy telling me this afternoon that the head of bookkeeping was about to quit because of that newfangled computer? I probably should go up there and check it out anyway. So what do you say?"

Things were happening so fast. All she knew was that she was going away with Mac, and instead of being frightened, she was suddenly thrilled at the idea of spending more time with him.

She wanted to find her grandfather, but she also wanted to be with Mac, and get to know him better. Yet she felt terribly guilty for feeling so happy. Was it so wrong? she wondered. Should she just go on up there alone and stop whatever was happening between her and Mac?

No! her mind shouted. Didn't she deserve at least one precious memory? And if one memory was all she was to have as the lonely years unfolded, then she wanted that memory to be of Mac. Dear, sweet, wonderful Mac.

For the first time in her life, because of him, she felt beautiful, cherished and cared for. Shouldn't every woman feel this way at least once in her life?

"Addy?" Mac prompted. "What do you say, are we going to Reno?" He looked so hopeful that Addy smiled and linked her arm through his.

"When do we leave?"

Mac expelled a sigh of relief. He had been afraid she'd say no, afraid he wouldn't have a chance to prove to her all the things he wanted to prove to her—the most important of which was that he loved her and needed her.

"First thing in the morning," he assured her, bending to brush his lips across hers. "First thing in the morning."

Chapter Six

The next morning, bright and early just as Mac had promised, Addy found herself standing stock-still, staring mutely at the private plane waiting to whisk them away to Reno.

"But, Mac," she protested feebly, raising her frightened eyes to his. "When you said we'd take a *ride* up there, I just assumed you meant...in a *car*," she finished lamely, trying to ignore the bemused smile on his face. Although, considering the way Mac drove, perhaps they would be safer in a plane—providing it didn't leave the ground.

"Addy," Mac said patiently. "There's nothing to be afraid of. You flew to Nevada and you weren't scared then, were you?"

"Petrified," she confessed, staring glumly at the giant silver monster with the Parkland emblem emblazoned on it. "But I had no choice. It was an emergency. I just took my seat, closed my eyes and didn't open them again until we were safely on the ground."

Mac chuckled softly. Taking her arm, he half pushed, half pulled her toward the entrance ramp, which had been lowered for their arrival.

"Mac." Swallowing hard, Addy came to an abrupt halt and wiped a bead of perspiration from her forehead. "No. I can't." A commercial airline was different, this... this... contraption was a small private plane, and she had no idea how or if it would stay up in the air—and she had no desire to find out. She stared at Mac morosely. "If I was meant to fly, I would have been born with a snubbed nose and silver wings."

Mac's laughter was lost amid the roar of the engines as the plane came to life, causing Addy to cower even closer to him. "Addy," he said softly, taking her hand and pulling her along. He kept up a running line of dialogue. "Do you trust me?" he asked, causing her to look up at him tentatively.

"Y... yes," she said, unsuccessfully trying to slow her steps as they drew closer to the plane.

"Do you think I'd let anything happen to you?" Setting her suitcase on the ground, Mac turned to her, his gaze pinning hers.

For a moment Addy stared at him, lost in the depths of his eyes and almost forgetting what she was afraid of. "No," she finally whispered as Mac's hands slowly drifted to her shoulders.

"Come on, now," he prompted, drawing her forward. He kept his hands on her shoulders, walking backward as he guided her toward the ramp. "Let's get on the plane. I'll be with you. I wouldn't let anything happen to you, Addy. And besides, I've got the best pilot in the business. I trained him myself." By the time he finished talking, he had her up the ramp and in the cabin. Not once did he take his eyes off her. His hands were warm and gentle on her shoulders as he coaxed her into a plush velvet chair. "Now, I'll be right here next to you. You can close your eyes if you want. You can even squeeze my hand if it makes you feel better.''

Addy paled a bit as she drew her gaze from his for a moment to glance out the window. The plane was moving. "Mac?" Her voice trembled and he quickly reached across her and snapped down the shade.

"Look at me, Addy," he soothed, taking her hands again. "It's less than an hour. You can make it, come on, I know you can." He'd keep talking the whole time if need be, anything to erase the fear from her huge green eyes. Her palms were damp, and he noticed she was trembling.

"Mac," she began again, but he raised a hand to stop her. If he could just keep her occupied until they were airborne, he was sure she'd be all right.

"It's okay," he soothed, pressing her head into his shoulder and silently willing the pilot to get the plane off the ground. He'd had enough experience with terrified flyers to know how easily they were spooked. Rosie would walk six days in the desert before she'd willingly get on a plane. She had taken a cruise to Hawaii rather than risk flying. He'd done his share of coaxing and conning Rosie when the need arose, but somehow with Addy, it was different. He wanted to take away all her fears; he wanted her to feel safe and protected when she was with him. And he'd do everything in his power to see that she was.

Mac fastened both their seat belts, then leaned back in his chair as the plane soared high in the air, heaving a sigh of relief as Addy seemed to relax against him. Fear usually subsided once the plane was up in the air. The next moment of terror would be the landing, but if he knew Chip, his pilot, it would be so smooth Addy would hardly notice. She lifted her head, and Mac was relieved to see some of the color flood back into her face.

"Feeling better?" he inquired, smiling at her.

She returned his smile. "Yes. And no. What I was trying to tell you back there, Mac, was that you left my suitcase on the ground." Addy chuckled at the look on his face.

"Oh, Lord, Addy, I'm sorry." He dragged a hand through his hair and burst out laughing. "I was so worried about getting you on the plane, I completely forgot about getting your suitcase on. But don't worry, the lower level of the Reno Parkland has a full shopping complex. We'll be able to buy anything you'll need." She frowned a bit and Mac rushed on. "Don't worry, it's on me. It's the least I can do after leaving all your things behind." She opened her mouth to protest, but Mac stopped her. "No arguing, now. It's my fault, and the least I can do. Besides, how much can it be to pick up a few days' worth of clothes? Now, I won't take no for an answer." He took her hand in his, and she forgot all about her protests.

She knew it would do no good anyway. Mac had that determined tilt to his jaw. She'd only seen it twice before— once when he told her he couldn't help her, and then again when he insisted he was going to help her. All in all, considering how short a time she had known Mac, she knew a great deal about him.

Mac kept up a steady flow of conversation from that point on, easing all of Addy's tension. When he announced they were in Reno, she was shocked. She never even felt the plane hit the ground.

"Mac, it's beautiful," Addy breathed as the limo pulled into the long winding driveway of the Reno Parkland. The hotel was smaller than the one in Vegas, and although Reno still had the required glitter, there was something homier about it. Addy fell in love with the town immediately.

The blazing sun and bright splashes of flowers and palm trees were so far removed from the landscape in Indiana,

Addy found herself totally entranced. It was as if she had landed in another world.

Mac helped her out of the car and led her under the glittering brick archway of the hotel. Although the building itself seemed a bit older than the Vegas hotel, there was a quaintness about the place that in some ways reminded Addy of home.

"Mr. Cole." A slender, immaculately dressed bellman appeared, smiling broadly. "It's good to see you again, sir."

"Thank you, James. This is Adeline Simpson."

"Miss Simpson." James nodded his head. "Your suite has been readied for your arrival, sir, and if you'll just follow me, I'll handle your luggage and show you to your suite."

"No luggage," Mac said, glancing at Addy. They both smiled.

If James thought it strange that they had no belongings, it didn't show in his face. Bowing grandly, he led them through the lobby and the crowded casino to a bank of private elevators at the far end of the hotel. Producing a key from his pocket, he inserted it into the elevator panel, and soon they were being whisked to the penthouse.

As James opened the door, Addy gasped. The room was spectacular. Three walls of glass allowed for a breathtaking view of the landscape twenty-five stories below. She could see the mountains off in the distance, capped by small tufts of white snow. As far as she could see were crystal blue skies and sunshine.

James discreetly dismissed himself as Addy made her way around the luxurious suite. The rooms were done in shades of white and gold. Her heels made soft clicking noises on the marble floor when she walked, so she slipped off her shoes and padded around in her bare feet. The rest of the suite was carpeted in thick luxurious white carpeting, complementing the ornate furniture.

"Mac, it's beautiful," she commented, walking to the window for another glance at the view.

He came up behind her and slipped his arms around her waist, drawing her close. She could feel the warmth of his body all the way down to her bare toes.

"I'm glad you like it, Addy," he said, burying his nose in her hair. He inhaled deeply, loving the wonderful feminine scent of her. "There's two bedrooms, each with their own adjoining bath. On the balcony off the master bedroom, you'll find a Jacuzzi that's always a pleasant 110 degrees. Anything you want, all you have to do is pick up that phone. James will get you anything you need."

She turned to face him. His pupils dilated and Addy's breath caught. Mac was so close she could feel his sweet breath brush the tender tendrils of hair at her temples. Without thinking, Addy reached up and gently brushed her lips across his.

The moment their lips met, she felt a rush of need unlike anything she had ever experienced before she met Mac. So many pleasures, so many sensations. They were things she'd only dreamed about, but because of Mac, now she was experiencing them.

If this was going to be her one reckless memory, she wanted to make it one to last a lifetime. She was going to do all the things she'd never done, much less thought of, and she wanted to do them with Mac.

His lips covered hers possessively as he tightened his arms around her, pulling her close. Addy sighed dreamily as she wrapped her arms around Mac.

Slowly he held her away from him. His breathing was short and erratic. "Addy, I think we'd better see about getting you some clothes. You'll need something to wear for dinner. Then I'll check in with security about your grandfather."

He took her hand and headed toward the door.

* * *

"Mac," Addy pleaded as he moved from rack to rack in the fashionable boutique, pulling out a blouse from here, a dress from there and a skirt from yet another. He bundled all his choices into the arms of a waiting saleswoman, much to Addy's distress. "I don't need all these things," she complained, following him around a bend in the elaborately decorated shop. "That poor woman's got more clothes in her arms than I have in my closets back home."

Paying her no mind, Mac kept moving through the store. He had vowed to give Addy all the things in life she had missed, and one thing was beautiful clothing. A woman like Addy was made for silk and lace, for satin slippers and cashmere sweaters. Not for drab clothing in boring colors, no matter how much she protested.

Other than an occasional birthday or Christmas gift for his sister or Hildy, Mac had never shopped for a woman before. He found to his delight that he was enjoying himself.

"Mac," Addy growled, trying to grab his arm. He stopped so abruptly she nearly crashed into him.

"Now this," he said, lifting a white beaded silk dress from the rack and holding it aloft, "is exactly what we've been looking for."

"We?" Addy cried, horrified when she caught a glimpse of the price. "Oh no you don't, MacArthur," she said, trying to snatch the gown from his hands. He held it high in the air so she couldn't reach it. "Buying me a few items to keep me going until we get back to Vegas is one thing, but this..." She waved her hand toward the white silk creation. "*This* is something else." She peeked at the price tag again and nearly choked. "Mac," she hissed again, trying to keep her voice low so the salesladies wouldn't overhear. "I've never spent that much money on a dress in my life.

I've never *had* that much money in my life," she amended with a frown.

Although the dress was lovely—in fact, it was probably the most beautiful dress she had ever seen—that didn't mean she was about to let Mac buy it for her. He was getting a bit too carried away with this picking-out-a-few-things-for-her stuff. She had no intention of taking advantage of his generous nature, no matter what the reason.

"Mmm," Mac said thoughtfully, a mysterious smile on his face as he put the dress atop the salesgirl's pile.

"Mac," Addy warned as he took off down another aisle. They were attracting a great deal of attention. Addy hadn't realized that as the owner of the Parkland, Mac would obviously be recognized. If he expected people to believe the story they'd concocted about her being there to sort out the bookkeeping problems, his current behavior must certainly seem suspicious.

After another fifteen minutes of frantic clothes grabbing, Mac sent her into one of the dressing rooms to try everything on. There were lightweight cotton skirts with matching blouses and sweaters, beautiful linen dresses and slacks, and of course, the dress.

When Addy tried it on, she couldn't believe her eyes. Beaded white silk draped from spaghetti straps of pearls to cover her small bosom in a crisscross design, and then blossomed to a flow of silk swirls. The back of the dress fell almost to the floor, tapering upward until it barely brushed her knees in front. The beads were pearls and sequins and reminded Addy of the dress the dancers wore in the stage show. Except this was no stage show production, this was a dress meant to be worn by a *beautiful* woman.

Addy stared at her reflection wistfully. This was the kind of dress she had always dreamed of owning, the kind of dress that made her feel beautiful and feminine.

"Addy? Are you decent?" Mac knocked on the door, then poked his head into the dressing room without waiting for a response.

"Mac!" she cried, not certain she wanted him to see her in this dress, particularly when she had no intention of getting it, no matter how lovely it was. She was not about to take advantage of Mac or his apparent generosity.

"Addy," he whispered. Mac inhaled slowly. His eyes widened as they met hers in the mirror. The gaze was so tender, so reverent, Addy's eyes filled with moist tears. Mac was looking at her the way she had always dreamed a man would look at her. "My God," he whispered. "You're beautiful."

"The dress is beautiful," she corrected.

"No, Addy," he said softly, stepping into the room and paying no mind to the scattering of clothes laying about. "*You're* beautiful. You and that dress were meant for each other." He took her in his arms, not caring that several salesladies were peeking around the corner, trying to see what was going on. "You're beautiful," he repeated, bending to brush his lips across hers.

Addy allowed Mac to draw her into his arms, knowing that time was going by all too quickly. Soon, all too soon, she would have to say goodbye to him. The thought brought a sudden pang to her heart, and she wrapped her arms around him and hugged him fiercely. She had never met anyone like him before and knew she would never meet anyone like him again. But one thing she did know. In just a short span of time she had fallen head over heels in love with the wonderful MacArthur Cole.

"Now, get changed," Mac ordered, setting her away from him. "We've got a couple other things to do. Just leave everything where it is. The salesladies will send them to our suite."

"But, Mac—"

"No buts, Addy, we're taking everything." At the look on her face, he rushed on. "Including the white dress. I have something special planned for that dress," he added mysteriously, stepping out of the dressing room and leaving Addy wondering.

In a few moments she had changed into her own clothes and was once again being led around the shopping arcade by Mac. "I've got a few things to take care of—"

"About Grandpa?" she asked hopefully, and Mac nodded. This time it wasn't a lie. Blackie had left an urgent message for him, and Mac hadn't had time to get back to him.

"Yes, about your grandfather. Now, I'm going to deliver you into the care of some people, and I want you to do whatever they say. All right?"

Addy glanced at him suspiciously as he led her through an oak door. "What people?"

"These people."

Addy turned to find herself face-to-face with about seven smiling individuals, all dressed in identical pink smocks.

"What is this place?" she whispered to Mac, who was busy smiling and shaking hands all around.

"It's a private health spa, Addy. I thought you might like a chance to relax a bit before dinner. Now, you run along, I've got things to do. I'll meet you back up in the suite by six." Without giving her a chance to protest, Mac turned on his heel and retreated through the door, leaving Addy alone to face the smiling seven.

For the next few hours, Addy was steamed, pummeled, massaged and pampered. After her body had been prepared by expert hands, she was turned over to the resident makeup artist, who went to work on her face. Wide-eyed, Addy stared in the mirror as the man changed her from a clean, fresh-faced woman into a sultry siren. He put a little bit of this here and a dab of that there. By the time he was finished, Addy barely recognized the woman in the mirror. She knew somewhere underneath all that makeup was the real Addy, but for right now, she was enjoying the woman she had become.

Finally she was turned over to Phyllis, the hairdresser, who oohed and aahed over her luxurious blond mane. She washed Addy's hair, then made her close her eyes as she snipped away with scissors. Fearing the worst, Addy refused to open her eyes until the woman was completely finished. When she did, she sat for a full five minutes with her mouth open.

Her blond hair was still shoulder length, but the sides and bangs had been feathered and cut, then curled up and away from her face, making her eyes seem even wider and her cheekbones more pronounced.

Addy continued to stare at her reflection. She reminded herself of someone, but she didn't know who. Then it struck her. For the first time in her life, she looked as beautiful as her mother. With her heart bursting, Addy thanked each and every one of the smiling seven, who gave her a standing ovation as she gathered her things and headed up to the suite. It was almost six and she couldn't wait to see Mac's reaction when he saw her.

Humming to herself, Addy let herself into the suite, only to find it empty. Mac had left her a note, along with a pitcher of lemonade, telling her to be dressed and ready when he returned. She glanced at her watch and realized she had barely ten minutes to change. There was no question in her mind what she would wear. Tonight was going to be special, Mac had said so himself. And Addy knew she wanted it to be a night to remember.

"Mac, say something!" She stood looking at him, her heart thudding wildly in anticipation. She had changed carefully so as not to mess her hair. She had found two

brand-new bottles of perfume on the dresser, obviously left there by Mac. One was heavenly and she had liberally splashed herself with it. After slipping on the white beaded dress, as well as the white silk shoes they had purchased to go with it, she sat down to wait for Mac.

When she heard his key in the door, her pulse had throbbed with excitement. Addy had waited until she was certain he was inside, before making her entrance. The soft carpeting had concealed her footsteps and when she called his name, he whirled around, his eyes rounding in total surprise. He had been standing there openmouthed for the past few minutes, not saying a word, but looking awfully uncomfortable shifting from foot to foot and staring at her.

"MacArthur," she said tightly, suddenly feeling an attack of nerves. What if her hair was all wrong, or her makeup or the dress? What if he liked her better the other way? Merciful Heaven, what if he didn't like the new her at all?

"Addy?" He took a step closer. "Is that you?" He took her gently by the hands and spun her slowly around so that he could get a good look at her. She'd always been beautiful to him, but now she was breathtaking. Did she know what she was doing to him? he wondered, looking into her wide emerald eyes.

He saw a question in her gaze and realized she was waiting for his approval. He'd been so caught up in his response to her, so involved in his own private needs, he forgot to tell her how stunning she looked.

"You look beautiful. Breathtaking," he added, turning her around again until she laughed softly. If Mac had any doubt before, now he had none. It wasn't the dress or the new hairdo or even the makeup, which he couldn't care less about. It was Addy that he wanted, and not just for a few days or a few nights—but for the rest of his life. How on earth was he going to tell her, convince her that he loved her and wanted her, when all along he'd been lying to her and deceiving her? Mac vowed that somehow he'd find a way. Somehow, someway, he'd make her understand. He had planned to do it tonight, to talk to her and try to explain things, but now... Circumstances had changed, and he wasn't sure this was the right time. One thing he did know for certain—he had waited his whole life for Miss Adeline Simpson, and he wasn't about to let her slip away. Not now, not ever. No matter what he had to do, he'd find a way to make her understand.

"This calls for a celebration," he said, dropping her hands to head for the phone. "You're much too beautiful to share with anyone. Tonight, I want you all to myself."

Addy shivered with delight and anticipation as Mac ordered dinner sent to the room. When he was finished, he flipped a switch and soft music drifted through the suite.

"I'm going to take a quick shower and change. But don't go away. I'll be right back." Mac kissed her quickly then retreated to his bedroom.

Addy touched her lips, still marveling at her immediate reaction to Mac. It didn't go away. Every time he touched her or even came near her, her nerves went into a tizzy. This was how love was supposed to feel, Addy realized, knowing instinctively what she felt for Mac was love.

Maybe she hadn't known him as long as Pernall, but what she felt for Mac was deeper and stronger than what she felt for a man she'd known her whole life. She loved Mac. The thought awed her and frightened her. When she left Muncie to find her grandfather, never in her wildest dreams had she thought she would find love instead.

Addy went to stand by the windows, watching as the fading sun cast a fiery orange glow across the mountainside. It was so beautiful, she thought wistfully. Everything. The suite, the view, everything about the past few days was beautiful, and she wanted to remember and savor each and every detail, to keep it safe within her heart.

"Addy, how about some champagne?" Mac emerged from the bedroom fresh from his shower. His hair was still damp and fell recklessly around his face. He wore slim gray slacks and a white dress shirt. He had left the shirt open at the collar, and he had rolled up his sleeves to reveal tanned forearms.

"Champagne?" Addy was thoughtful for a moment. "Yes," she said with a laugh. "I'd love some." Tonight truly was going to be a celebration, a beautiful wonderful memory she was going to cherish forever.

Mac had just finished pouring the pale liquid into fluted glasses when there was a knock at the door. After handing Addy her glass, he went to the door.

Three elegantly dressed waiters appeared, pushing in a table elaborately set for dinner. Addy sipped her champagne as she watched the men set up the table right near the window so they would be able to see the view while they ate.

Once the men had left, Mac held out a chair for her, then scooted his own chair closer to hers. Lifting his glass, he looked deep into her eyes.

"Addy, a toast. To you, for making the past few days the happiest of my life." His gaze snared hers and Addy's heart stilled.

"Oh, Mac." Her fingers trembled on her glass as she lifted it into the air. "No, Mac, this toast is for you. The past few days have been the happiest of *my* life. And I want to thank you for your kindness, and for the wonderful memories," she added softly, glancing away. "I won't ever forget these past few days."

"Hey," Mac said, reaching out to squeeze her hand. "Don't sound so glum. You make it sound like it's over. Things are just beginning."

Hope flared and Addy wondered exactly *what* was beginning between them. At the moment, it was too precious to try to name.

"Well," she began, deciding to change the subject. "I just want you to know how much I appreciate all your help. I don't know what I would have done if you hadn't offered to help me find my grandfather." A sudden thought occurred to her. "Did you learn anything this afternoon?"

Mac set his glass down slowly. "A few things," he hedged, unable to look into her trusting green eyes.

"Do you think we'll find him soon, Mac?"

Mac nodded. Her voice sounded so hopeful, so expectant, Mac averted his gaze, suddenly feeling ashamed. "I have a feeling, Addy, that by tomorrow at this time we'll know exactly where he is." He didn't want to talk about Blackie or the casino or anything else right now. What he wanted to do was enjoy the evening with Addy. He glanced down at their covered dishes. "Let's eat before our food gets cold." Mac removed the silver cover, but barely ate. He just kept pushing his food around the plate.

He had made up his mind to tell Addy the truth tonight. He didn't want to lie to her anymore. He wanted her to know how he felt about her; he wanted her to know that what he had done had not been out of cruelty, but out of a determined effort to help. But when he had returned Blackie's urgent call, Mac had been shocked by the news Blackie had for him. Blackie had discovered the identity of two of the culprits bilking the casino, and Mac was distressed to learn they were employees of the Parkland. Blackie was certain there was at least one other person involved, maybe more.

The news sent Mac into a tailspin. This wasn't just a simple case of a con now, but something much, much more. He had no idea if there were other employees involved, or if this was just a two-person operation. In either case, it meant trouble, serious trouble, not just for him, but possibly for the Parkland, as well.

The Nevada Gaming Control Board took a very dim view of casino pilfering, regardless of who was responsible. If Mac didn't find out who and how many were responsible for the shenanigans, it was possible he could become suspect. If that was the case, he could not only lose his gaming license, but his casino, too.

The thought of losing the hotels, as well as his livelihood, weighed heavily on his mind. He had a responsibility to the thousands of honest employees. If the hotel chain was closed down for gaming violations, what would happen to all the people who depended on Mac for a paycheck?

Lord, what a mess. Thank goodness he had called Blackie when he did, or else who knew how long and how far this thing could have gone? Blackie had promised he would have some final answers by tomorrow. Mac knew he couldn't tell Addy the truth tonight, he just couldn't. He had to let Blackie finish what he started. He'd have to wait one more day and hope like hell he'd be able to make her understand.

"Mac? Mac? Is something wrong?" Addy was watching him carefully. He'd been acting strange ever since he came up to the suite.

"What?" Blinking, Mac brought his attention back to Addy and smiled. He'd been lost in his own private world for a few moments.

"I said, is something wrong?"

"No, I was just thinking." He lifted his glass and took a sip of champagne, watching her carefully over the rim.

Addy laid down her fork. "About what?"

"About you." She glanced away for a moment, suddenly uncomfortable, but Mac continued. "That dress is beautiful, and so is your hair and makeup. But you know what, Addy? Underneath it all, you're still the same person, the same beautiful person you were. All that stuff—"

Mac gestured with his hand "—none of it makes one bit of difference. Oh, it changes the outside packaging a bit, but it doesn't change what you are inside." He reached across the table and covered her hand with his. "Do you understand what I'm saying?"

Addy brought her gaze back to his and nodded her head. She finally did understand. She had learned so much the past few days, not just about herself, but about life. For too long she had allowed herself to bury her dreams. She'd allowed her guilt over her mother's death to get all tangled up with her feelings of who she was and what she was supposed to do.

Addy knew one thing. Maybe she wasn't as beautiful as her mother, and maybe she never would be, but it suddenly didn't matter anymore. Mac had taught her that outer beauty meant nothing. *Inner* beauty was what counted. Mac was right. While she was pleased with her new, more glamorous look, it didn't change who or what she was on the inside. Inside, she was still Adeline Simpson from Muncie, Indiana.

She also finally realized that there was more to life than Muncie and Pernall. She'd never dared dream that she could have more; it had seemed selfish. But now Addy knew there was a lot more to life than what she'd been willing to settle for. And that, too, Mac had taught her.

She'd been touched by love, so how could she ever settle for anything less? She knew she couldn't. How could she spend her life in a town she didn't like with a man she didn't love?

Addy couldn't. A few days ago she could have, but that was before she had come face-to-face with a mountain of a man who touched her life and her heart with his love and his kindness.

She was going to have to let Pernall down gently. But Addy knew she could never marry him, not now, not knowing how she felt about Mac. It wouldn't be right, and it certainly wouldn't be fair to Pernall. *Nor to her.* Pernall deserved more, but so did she. She didn't know how she was going to tell Pernall, but she'd figure out a way.

And she also didn't know how she was going to get the money to pay the taxes on Simpson House, but was sure that somehow she'd find a way. And if she didn't, then she'd sell it. She'd been hanging on to the house as some sort of connection to her mother. She'd been doing it to gain her mother's approval, but she had come to terms with the fact that it was too late, not just for her, but for her mother, as well. She no longer *needed* her mother's approval. The knowledge seemed to unlock her from the prison of her past.

Addy realized she was her own person, with her own feelings and desires. Though she may not have turned out to be what her mother wanted, she was happy with who she was and what she was, and finally, Addy realized, it was enough.

It was a shame it had taken her so long to learn, she thought. She could have saved herself a lot of heartache and grief. So many years wasted; so much sadness and misery.

Perhaps by opening up to Mac the other night, she had opened the dam. Now that all the pain and all her fears had been verbalized, they didn't seem to have the power to hurt her anymore. It was time to stop living in her mother's shadow, time to stop feeling guilty for things she couldn't control. It was time for her to start living her life the way she wanted to. The past was gone and she could do nothing to change it. But what she could do was change her future—if she wanted to. And Addy realized she did.

As long as she had Grandpa and Aunt Myrtle, what difference did it make where they lived? And Mac. Dear Mac. She glanced at him. No matter what happened, Addy knew she was going to cherish these moments with Mac, because he had taught her something she would never forget. Mac had taught her *she was worth something*. For the first time in her life, Addy realized she *deserved* happiness. She only wished that things were different and that she could be with Mac.

She loved him and was no longer willing to *settle* for things; she was ready to go after what she wanted in life. And what she wanted most of all was Mac.

"Dance with me?" she said abruptly, holding out her hand to him. Mac took her hand and slowly drew her to her feet. The music was soft and slow. Addy went into Mac's arms, nestling her head against his shoulder as he led her around the room.

"Addy?" Mac whispered against her hair. "I . . . I want to talk to you about something."

She lifted her head to look at him, smiling dreamily. "What?"

Mac frowned, wondering how he was going to get this out. It was so important he didn't want to screw it up. "Now, I know we haven't known each other very long, and I know you're supposed to be thinking over Parsnips's marriage proposal—"

"Pernall," she said, laughing softly and laying her head back down on his shoulder. "But tonight, I don't want to talk about Pernall, or anything else," she whispered, moving closer to him. "Tonight, I just want to enjoy being with you."

Mac frowned again. He wasn't handling this very well. "Addy?"

"Hmm?"

"What would you say if I told you that . . . that . . ."

Addy lifted her head and looked at Mac, wondering why he appeared so distressed. "Mac, what is it? What are you trying to say?" They stared at each other for a long, silent moment. Eyes locked, they seemed to speak more than words ever could express. Addy knew in her heart that what she felt at the moment was what she had waited for her whole life.

"I love you," she whispered. The world seemed to stand still for a heartbeat as Addy watched Mac's reaction. His eyes darkened for one brief moment, and she saw a wave of emotion flicker across his face before he hauled her into his arms.

"Oh, Addy." Mac pulled her closer, pressing the warmth of her body against him. "I love you, too. *I love you,*" he whispered fiercely, his heart bursting with joy.

Wrapped in the warmth and security of Mac's arms and his love, Addy's heart soared. She had waited for this her whole life. But now it seemed as if her life was just beginning. The past was over—gone—there was nothing she could do to change it, but what she could do was accept it. Mac's love gave her the courage to try. Today would be the beginning of a new life and a new love.

"I love you," she whispered again. Joy filled her as Mac's arms tightened around her.

"I love you, too," Mac said fiercely. "I love everything about you. And I never, ever, want anything or anyone to hurt you again."

Smiling, Addy lifted her head to look at him. She never thought it possible to feel so happy, so content, so peaceful.

"There are so many things we have to talk about, Mac." Shaking her head, she laughed softly. "I came to Las Vegas to find my grandfather. Instead, I found love."

His mouth took hers possessively, moving with a heat that engulfed them both.

A rapid knock at the door startled them and Mac swore softly. "Damn. I told them we weren't to be disturbed." He moved out of Addy's arms and toward the door. "This better be important," Mac growled as he ripped the door open. An ashen-looking James stood on the other side, twisting his hands together.

"Mr. Cole, please—" the man swallowed hard at the look on Mac's face "—please, forgive the intrusion. I know you left orders not to be disturbed but . . ." He glanced at Addy over Mac's shoulder. "But could I have a bit of a word with you? Outside?"

Mac glanced at James, then back at Addy. "I'll be right back," he said, stepping out and shutting the door behind him. If James disturbed him, it had to be important.

A moment later, Mac walked back into the room, looking distracted and a bit pale.

"Mac?" Addy said in alarm, going to him. "What's wrong? Is it Grandpa?"

"Addy," he began calmly, "I don't want you to get upset, but we have to go back to Vegas. *Now.*" He tried to keep the urgency out of his voice.

"Now!" she cried in confusion. Mac grabbed the phone. She couldn't make out his words, but she had a feeling he was making arrangements for their flight back. "But we just got here!" she protested, wondering what had happened to the beautiful evening they had planned.

"I know, hon," Mac said, putting the phone down and turning to her. He didn't want to alarm her. "We have a bit of an emergency at the casino in Vegas, and I think I'm going to need your help."

She frowned. "My help?" What on earth could she possibly do to help him? She didn't know anything about the casino business. "Mac, please, tell me what's wrong."

He glanced at his watch. "We have exactly fifty-five minutes to get back."

"Wait a minute. What about my new clothes—what about dinner—what about tonight?"

"Leave your clothes. James will send them later. We'll grab a bite to eat on the plane. We'll have plenty of time to talk later. Now, hurry, Addy."

"I'm not going anywhere until you tell me what's wrong!" Addy stood stock-still, refusing to budge until Mac gave her some information. He dragged a hand through his hair.

"Addy, about fifteen minutes ago a woman walked into the Parkland casino—with a pigeon on her arm. She said that she'd been trying to reach her niece for two days, and unless someone produced her in exactly one hour, she's . . . Well, Addy, it looks like she's holding my casino hostage— with a pigeon!"

Chapter Seven

Aunt Myrtle?'' Addy sank to the sofa. "What on earth is she doing here?'' She raised her eyes to his, suddenly alarmed. "Why would she come?''

Mac shook his head. "I don't know, hon. She must be pretty upset about something.''

"But you don't understand, Mac, Walter *hates* to fly!''

Mac bit back a smile. He didn't have time to ponder the incongruity of a pigeon who didn't like to fly. He was about to have mass hysteria on his hands if Myrtle let that pigeon loose in his casino. He could just imagine his staff trying to cope with this little catastrophe. Lord, where was Rosie when he needed her?

"I know, honey, but, let's not try to guess the reasons why,'' he said trying to soothe her. "Let's just get back and ask her ourselves.''

"Mac,'' Addy quickly got to her feet as the vision of Aunt Myrtle and Walter slowly drifted through her mind. "The guards, what about the guards? How are they taking this?''

Addy frowned deeply. "Merciful Heaven!" She remembered how the security guards had pounced on her, and she could just imagine how they would react to Aunt Myrtle and Walter, who weren't exactly the garden variety Las Vegas tourists. "They won't hurt her, will they?" The thought caused her to panic.

Mac smiled. "No, Addy. I had James tell them they were not to touch her or alarm her. They're just going to try and keep her . . . company until we get there." He didn't bother to tell her he had instructed the guards to sequester Myrtle and her fine feathered friend in a secluded spot and keep them there until he arrived. He drew Addy into his arms. "Don't worry, she'll be fine. And so will Walter. As long as I produce you."

"It must be something awfully important for her to come all this way," Addy said, deep in thought. "You don't know her, Mac, but it would take a lot for Aunt Myrtle—and Walter—to do something like this." Addy shook her head. "It's just so unlike her." Aunt Myrtle had been known to do some strange things, but this was strange even for her! "Mac." Addy's frown deepened. "You don't think she's heard something about Grandpa? You don't think it's bad news?"

Mac shook his head, trying to calm Addy's fears. "How could she have heard something from him when we can't even *find* him? And why wouldn't she just have telephoned? No, hon, I think you're just jumping to conclusions. But rather than speculate, let's go find out what she wants." Mac dragged a hand through his hair. "You see, Addy, she made her . . . *demands* . . . very clear. Unless she sees *you*—within the hour—she's planning on wreaking holy havoc on my casino. Addy, I don't know how to tell you this, but letting a pigeon loose in the Parkland isn't exactly going to win me points with the Nevada Gaming Control Board." Mac smiled gently. "You see, sweetheart, something like this, well, they could close me down." He tried to keep the concern out of his voice. Addy was worried enough without him adding to her problems, but he wanted her to know the importance of this.

"Mac, I'm sorry. I never gave a thought to the consequences, I've just been so concerned with myself." She smiled sheepishly and dropped her arms around his neck. "That's one of the things I love about you. I did tell you I loved you, didn't I?" she whispered, brushing her lips across his and causing Mac to groan softly.

"Yes," he whispered, accepting the softness of her kiss. "But not nearly enough."

Addy drew away, suddenly shaken. "I think we'd better get going," she said softly, a faint hue of pink touching her cheeks. Mac nodded as he hustled her toward the door.

"Addy?" Mac said cautiously as he started toward the elevators. "Aunt Myrtle...she...she wouldn't *really* let Walter loose, would she?"

Addy's expression grew doubtful. "I don't know, Mac. Aunt Myrtle isn't like most people." Her words caused Mac to frown. That, obviously, was an understatement. Not many people traveled around with a pigeon. "If she's threatening to let Walter loose..." She gave him a wan smile.

"Yes, but *will she do it*?" Mac persisted, trying to hurry Addy along.

"In a word?" She glanced up at him and tried not to smile at the look of suspense on his face. "Yes!"

They made the one-hour flight in exactly fifty-eight minutes. Addy had been too upset to worry about flying. She'd just shut her eyes and had squeezed Mac's hand. The only time she balked was when they landed at McCarran International Airport and Mac informed her they didn't have fifteen minutes to drive to the casino; he had arranged to have a helicopter standing by.

Before Addy could open her mouth to protest, Mac scooped her up in his arms and climbed aboard the whirlybird. Keeping Addy wrapped in his arms, he talked to her all the way to the casino. They made it in four and a half minutes flat, landing atop the heliport of the hotel.

As they alighted, a security guard was waiting. "Where is she?" Mac yelled, trying to be heard above the roar of the propellers.

"We've got her secured in the coffee shop," the guard said, opening a door for Mac and Addy to enter.

"Secured," Addy said in alarm. "Oh, Mac! Aunt Myrtle has quite a temper—when she remembers what she's mad about—and I wouldn't want to be those guards if they've made her angry."

The guard looked at Addy sheepishly. "No, ma'am. No one's touched a hair on her head. We just thought she'd be more comfortable in the coffee shop."

Taking her hand, Mac led Addy down a flight of steep stairs that led directly onto the penthouse floor that housed security and his office. He hustled her into the elevator, praying they had arrived in time.

The door to the elevator opened, and Addy raced through the casino with Mac right on her heels. She skidded to a halt as she came into the coffee shop.

"Aunt Myrtle," Addy cried, as her eyes landed on the thin birdlike woman calmly feeding chocolate chip cookie crumbs to a pigeon who sat perfectly posed on the arm of one of the burly security guards, much to the man's chagrin.

"Addy, darling, why there you are." Myrtle smiled. "Walter was just saying it was getting late and he was starting to worry. You know how he worries about you, dear." She continued feeding the pigeon, totally oblivious to the agonized look of the guard on whose arm Walter was perched. "Weren't you?" she cooed to the bird who gazed at her balefully.

"Aunt Myrtle, what are you doing here?" Addy knelt down and spoke directly into her aunt's calm face. She knew where her aunt was concerned it was best to get to the point—quickly.

"Why, I'm feeding Walter," Myrtle replied, causing Addy to take a deep breath. "And who is this young man you've got with you?" Myrtle inquired, giving Mac a long look, as well as a bright smile. "He's a big one, and quite handsome, if I do say so myself."

"Aunt Myrtle, this is Mac. MacArthur Cole. He's the man you told me might be able to help me find Grandpa, remember?"

From the look on Myrtle's face she clearly didn't remember any such thing. Myrtle extended one thin, bony hand. "It's nice to meet you, Arthur. You must be the reason for the sparkle in my niece's eye." Mac took the hand she offered.

"MacArthur," Addy quickly corrected, glancing sheepishly at Mac, who just smiled and took Myrtle's hand.

"It's nice to meet you, too," Mac said, not entirely sure that was the case, but being a sport about it anyway. This woman looked more like someone's grandma than a pigeon-armed terrorist. She was tiny and frail, with a thatch of snow-white hair that was piled atop her head in something resembling a bird's nest. She wore skinny, gold wireless glasses, and a floral-print dress that was definitely from another decade. She looked totally harmless, if a bit bewildered.

Myrtle continued to hold Mac's hand, looking up at him expectantly. She was obviously waiting for something. The problem was, Mac had no idea what.

"Addy?" he hissed. "What's she waiting for?"

"Say hello to Walter," Addy whispered.

"What?" Mac frowned.

"Say hello to Walter," Addy repeated. Mac stared at her blankly for a moment. Her green eyes softened. "Please?"

Trying to bank down a smile, Mac turned toward the pigeon and extended his hand, taking the pigeon's tiny claw between two fingers and shaking it properly. "Hello, Walter, it's nice to meet you."

There was a round of tittering from the guards, but Mac gave them a scathing look that put an end to any comments they had. If Addy wanted him to talk to a pigeon, he'd talk to a pigeon. If she wanted him to dance on the ceiling, he'd do that, too. He'd do anything for this woman, and he didn't care who knew it.

"That's better," Myrtle said, decidedly pleased. "Walter's so sensitive, you know. I've told him many times it's not good to be so sensitive. But he's a bit high-strung, I guess, and there's really nothing we can do about it. But we love you anyway, don't we, precious?" Myrtle cooed, feeding the bird another cookie crumb.

"Aunt Myrtle," Addy began, "would you please tell me why you're here, and why you threatened to let Walter loose in the casino unless someone produced me?"

Myrtle frowned, her silver brows drawing together behind her glasses. "Did *I* say that?" she asked in confusion. She glanced from Addy to the guards, who nodded their heads in confirmation. Myrtle giggled, raising a hand to her mouth. "Well, I guess I *did*, didn't I?" She leaned close to Addy. "Can't remember—exactly," she said in mild complaint. "But it'll come to me—eventually."

Mac rolled his eyes toward the heavens. Obviously this woman's batteries had burned down, but somehow he found her endearing. And the love between her and Addy was clear. Now if he could only figure out what she was doing here. He nudged Addy's shoulder.

"Aunt Myrtle, please tell me why you're here. Now, *think hard*. It must have been something very important for you to come all this way. I know how you hate to fly."

"Oh, dear, it's not me who hates to fly," Myrtle protested. "It's Walter. I think it's because of the time—"

"Yes, I know," Addy interrupted, "but *why* did you come?" Addy knew if she didn't keep her aunt's mind on track, another year could roll off the calendar before they ever figured out why she had come. From experience, Addy knew persistence, and a dose of good old-fashioned patience usually worked best.

"Mmm." Myrtle tapped her lip in confusion. She suddenly brightened. "I remember, now," she said, causing Addy and Mac to heave a sigh of relief. "I think," she added with a frown. Myrtle was quiet for a moment, then suddenly she turned to Addy and spoke in a hushed voice. "I'm afraid Walter's been a very naughty boy." Both Addy and Mac glanced at the bird. The guard on whose arm Walter was perched groaned softly, sneaking a peek at his shirt to be certain it wasn't *him* Walter had been *"naughty"* on.

"What did Walter do?" Addy asked, knowing her aunt's penchant for blaming Walter for things she didn't particularly want to 'fess up to.

"Well, let me see if I can remember all of this. I know it had something to do with yesterday—" she frowned again "—or was it the day before?" Myrtle shook her head. "Can't seem to recall, but I do know it had *something* to do with Mr. Ditkus."

"Pernall?" Addy's heart began to pound in fear. Oh, Lord. She had completely forgotten about him until this very moment. Her mind had been filled with nothing but Mac. Now reality reached up and slapped Addy back into the present.

"Aunt Myrtle," Addy took her aunt's hand. "*Please* try to remember. It's *very* important."

Mac dropped a comforting hand to Addy's shoulder. He didn't like the sudden tremor in her voice or the alarm in her face when she talked about this Parsnips guy. His dislike for the man grew in direct proportion to Addy's concern.

Myrtle muttered to herself for a few moments, leaving Addy and Mac to stare at each other in amazed wonder. Finally Myrtle slapped her hand to her forehead. "Now I remember," she declared, smiling broadly. "Yes, it was yesterday, wasn't it, Walter?" She waited a moment, for what, Mac didn't know, but apparently Myrtle and Walter had their own private language. "Yes, that's right, Walter, dear, I should have asked you first. You always did have a good memory."

"Aunt Myrtle," Addy prompted, wanting to get the information before her aunt forgot it again. "You were going to tell us what happened?"

"Oh, yes, that. Well, Walter and I were out having our afternoon walk with Mr. Merriman." She turned to Mac. "He's our neighbor and a dearer man you'll never find. Every afternoon about four he comes over and we take our afternoon stroll together. Addy doesn't like me going out alone and—"

"Aunt Myrtle," Addy cried, her patience strained to the limit now. "What happened with Pernall?"

"Well, I was just getting to that, dear. Anyway, when Mr. Merriman and I returned from our stroll, Mr. Ditkus was waiting for us on the steps." If Myrtle heard Addy's muffled groan, she didn't show it. "Anyway, Mr. Ditkus had called earlier in the day looking for you, and well..." She hesitated for a moment. "We knew you didn't want him to know you had gone to Las Vegas to look for Grandpa, so Walter told him you were down with a bad head cold. Silly Walter," she scolded, shaking her finger at the mute bird.

"He should have known Mr. Ditkus would come over to see how you were. Anyway, when we found him standing on the steps, we had no choice but to let him in. *That's* when Walter spilled the beans." She reached out a hand and stroked the furry creature. "It's all right, darling, we all make mistakes, don't we?"

"Spilled the beans?" Mac repeated, glancing from Addy to Myrtle in confusion.

"Well, it was clear to Mr. Ditkus that Addy wasn't home, and that Walter had told a little fib." Myrtle sighed heavily, causing the bosom of her dress to billow out before settling back down against her slender frame. "Anyway, Mr. Ditkus got a might upset. *Very* upset," she repeated, nodding her head knowingly.

Mac's hands tightened into fists. He didn't like the turn of this conversation, and he liked Parsnips Ditkus even less. If he harmed Myrtle, or touched one hair on her head, Mac would personally—

"What exactly did he do?" Addy asked nervously, causing Mac's anxiety level to rise. Why did just the sound of this guy's name cause Addy such distress? He had a feeling there was a lot more to this than she had led him to believe. And he was determined to get to the bottom of it—as soon as Myrtle finished her long-winded tale.

"Well, it's more what Walter did." She sighed again. "I'm afraid Walter became offended at the way Mr. Ditkus was talking to me. Mr. Ditkus started shouting, and you know how Walter hates loud noises." She clucked her tongue and shook her white head sadly. "It was then that it happened."

"Wait a minute," Mac said with a frown, holding up his hand. "Then *what* happened?" he asked, deciding the situation called for assertive intervention—his. Mac went down on one knee next to Addy so he could talk directly to Myrtle. He took one of her hands in his, trying to remain

calm. He didn't like what he was hearing. How could anyone shout at this dear old woman. Despite her character
flaws, or perhaps *because* of them, Mac found her instantly endearing. And he wasn't exactly pleased to hear that
Parsnips had been verbally abusive to her. Myrtle might be
slightly dotty, but she was about as defenseless as anyone
he'd ever met. Parsnips was beginning to sound more and
more like another man who verbally intimidated harmless
women. His stepfather.

"Myrtle," he began gently, waiting until he had her full
attention before going on. "I'm sorry Mr. Ditkus was rude
to Walter and raised his voice. I know something like that
can be frightening. And it certainly wasn't very respectful,
either. But if you'll just tell Addy and me what happened,
maybe we can help." He patted Myrtle's hand in assurance.
"We won't be mad at Walter, will we, Addy?" He glanced
at her and saw the smile on her face.

"No, Aunt Myrtle," she whispered softly, her eyes on
Mac. "We won't be mad." She laid a hand on his shoulder,
wanting to touch him at this moment. Mac was being so
kind, so gentle with her aunt. She couldn't help but com-
pare Mac's treatment of her aunt with Pernall's. Not many
men would have the patience to wait around until Aunt
Myrtle had it in her mind to get to the point. She felt an
overwhelming rush of love for Mac.

"So just tell us and we'll take care of it for you," Mac
added.

Myrtle looked at Mac for a long time, then finally sighed.
"I like you, young man. Very much. Are you married?" she
asked without breaking stride.

Mac chuckled softly. "No," he replied, glancing at Addy.
"Not yet."

Addy's heart soared at his words, but she cautioned herself not to read too much into them.

"Good." Myrtle's eyes sparkled mischievously. "Would you like to get married?" she asked coquettishly, causing Mac to grin. "It's been a long time since a gentleman held my hand, and in my day that usually meant we were engaged. But, I guess I'm a bit too old for you, although it would be nice for Walter to have a father."

"Aunt Myrtle," Addy prompted, trying not to smile. Obviously she wasn't the only one Mac was capable of charming. "What happened with Pernall?"

Myrtle frowned. "Oh, yes, that. I was hoping you'd forget. Well, Mr. Ditkus had poor Walter in such a dither, what with his yelling and screaming, Walter let it slip that you were here, in Las Vegas, looking for your grandfather. And then... then..." Myrtle looked at Mac sorrowfully.

"Then what, Myrtle?" he prompted gently, knowing whatever it was was causing her a great deal of distress.

"Then, well, dear, I'm afraid Walter lost his temper and bit him!"

"Merciful Heaven!" Addy muttered, dropping her head.

"Well, it wasn't a bite—" Myrtle frowned "—exactly. I'd say it was more like a little peck. And anyway, under the circumstances, what with Mr. Ditkus shouting and carrying on and all, you could hardly blame poor Walter. He's not used to so much excitement. Why, I had to put him down for his nap early because he'd been so distressed."

Grinning broadly, Mac reached out and stroked Walter, taking a liking to the feathered creature all of a sudden. "Good for you," he said, winking at Myrtle. Walter preened at Mac's praise.

"Please don't be angry with Walter, dear." Myrtle squeezed Addy's hand. "He didn't mean anything, and it really wasn't his fault."

"I'm not mad at Walter," Addy said softly, kissing her aunt's cheek. "And I'm not angry with you." Addy dragged up a wan smile. How could she tell her aunt that Walter biting Pernall was the last thing she was upset about? She should have known she would never have been able to keep her trip a secret from him. She should have just told him right from the beginning. But that still was no excuse for Pernall to take it out on her aunt. "Aunt Myrtle, please don't worry about it. You and Walter did nothing wrong. Pernall had absolutely no business yelling at either you or Walter. How dare he upset you like that!" Addy's temper began to simmer. Pernall knew how much Aunt Myrtle meant to her, but then again, just as he felt about her grandfather, Pernall never did care much for her aunt. He found her totally confusing, not to mention irritating. But that was certainly no reason for him to behave so rudely!

"Well, dear, I'm glad you're not angry at us. Walter was very concerned. Particularly when Mr. Ditkus told us..." Myrtle's eyes filled with tears and she blinked furiously.

"Told you what?" Mac and Addy caroled in unison.

Myrtle sniffed, wiping away a fallen tear with the back of her hand. "He told us that we weren't welcome in your life after you two were married. He said Walter should... should..." She hiccuped, then shook her head, unable to go on.

"Should what?" Mac prompted.

Myrtle reached out and covered Walter's ears. "Should be plucked and pureed," she whispered. Her eyes filled with tears again, and Mac shook his head. He had a feeling Myrtle wasn't telling them all of it.

"What else did he say?" Mac inquired.

Myrtle glanced away.

"Myrtle?"

She swallowed hard, and Mac could see her fighting to gain control of her tears. "He said we weren't... stable...and should be put away somewhere." Soft, silent sobs shook her slender frame. "That's why we left." Finally letting the tears come, Myrtle laid her head on Mac's shoulder and cried. His arms automatically went around her in comfort. Mac felt his insides tighten. The need to hit something—particularly Parsnips—was so strong Mac could hardly contain himself.

Walter let loose a squall that caused all eyes to turn in his direction, but Mac ignored everyone but the distressed woman sobbing against his shoulder.

"You were afraid," Mac confirmed, gently patting Myrtle's back. He could feel her frail body shake with tears, and his heart went out to her. His temper wasn't idle, either. If he ever laid eyes on Parsnips... He glanced at Addy and saw the fire blazing in her green eyes, saw the thin determined set of her mouth.

Addy's temper slowly exploded as she watched Mac comfort her aunt. Now she finally understood why Aunt Myrtle was here. She knew it had to be something pretty important for her and Walter to get on a plane, but the thought that Pernall had *frightened* Aunt Myrtle into coming had simply never occurred to her. How dare he treat her aunt in such a manner, or tell her that once they were married she and Walter were not welcome in her life! For too long Addy had been letting others decide her life's fate, but no more. *No more!*

"Aunt Myrtle?"

Myrtle lifted her head and looked up at Addy. Mac reached into his pocket and removed his handkerchief. Gently he lifted Myrtle's tearstained glasses off her nose and carefully dabbed at her eyes a bit before returning her glasses to their rightful place. She smiled at him, then patted his cheek.

"Look at me," Addy continued. "Aunt Myrtle, I want you to know that no matter what, you and Walter will always be welcome in my life. *Always.* Do you understand?"

"Are you sure, dear?" Myrtle asked, her eyes clouded with uncertainty. Addy smiled.

"I've never been surer of anything in my life. *I love you.* And Walter," she added hastily. "You're my family. I could never send you away. Not ever."

"The only one who should be put away is that Parsnips guy," Mac muttered, dragging his hand through his hair.

"Well, you might not feel that way once you hear the rest of it."

"The rest of it?" Addy sputtered.

"Dear," Myrtle said, looking at Addy over the rims of her glasses. "I'm afraid I haven't quite told you the worst part."

"You haven't?" Merciful Heaven, Addy thought, what could possibly be worse?

"I haven't," Myrtle confirmed. "Seems Mr. Ditkus got highly insulted that you would take off without so much as a how-de-do for him. Especially after Walter told him he had nothing to worry about, because you were coming here to get Mr. Cole to help you find Grandpa." Addy groaned, but her aunt plunged on. "Well, it seems that Mr. Ditkus told Walter that he...that he..." Myrtle sighed and wrung her hands together. "Addy, Mr. Ditkus is on his way here to Las Vegas. He's coming to get you!"

Chapter Eight

He's what!" Addy jumped to her feet, groaning silently. Merciful Heaven, this was all she needed.

"Didn't you hear me, dear?" Aunt Myrtle inquired, looking quite confused.

Addy patted her shoulder. "Yes, I heard you, Aunt Myrtle," Addy said glumly. "I just didn't believe you."

"Well, for goodness' sakes, why not?" Myrtle frowned, causing her glasses to slip down her nose. "You know I wouldn't lie to you, child."

Mac smiled at the befuddled woman before getting to his feet. "Addy, why don't we take your aunt and Walter back to the house? I'm sure she's had enough excitement for one day and would like some rest." He wanted Addy out of the casino. *Now.* If Parsnips really was on his way to find her, Mac wanted a chance to talk to Addy, to come clean with her about everything before she saw him.

He thought fleetingly about what Hildy would say about Walter. Hildy had only one rule in her house—nothing furry, feathered or four legged—no exceptions. He could just see her face when he showed up with Myrtle *and* Walter. Well, he couldn't worry about that now. He'd just have to try to explain the situation as best he could.

Mac helped Myrtle to her feet, then watched as the guards put Walter back into his cage. He escorted the ladies out of the casino into a waiting limo.

Myrtle and Walter seemed duly impressed with the plush car, and they settled back to enjoy the ride.

Addy was decidedly quiet. She stared glumly out the window, lost in thought. Mac left her alone; he figured she needed some time to sort things out in her own mind, just as he did. There would be plenty of time to talk tonight, to pick up where they had left off once they got Myrtle and Walter settled.

As the limo pulled into the long driveway, the front door opened. Hildy stood in the doorway, watching as they alighted from the car. As they approached the house, she took one look at Addy's ashen complexion, Myrtle's tear-stained face and Walter's cage, and said to Mac, "Judging from the looks of you, I suspect this little story can wait until morning." Without another word, Hildy took the bird cage in one hand and Myrtle in the other and marched them into the house, directly to the spare bedroom.

Mac paced the living room floor, wondering how he was going to say what he had to say. Addy watched him, curling up on the sofa and tucking her feet up under her.

"Addy," Mac began as he continued his pacing. "I realize a lot has happened in the past few days, but I want you to know something. I meant every word I said when we were in Reno. I do love you, and I think I have from the moment I found you in my office. I know we haven't known each other very long, but sometimes the length of time isn't nearly as important as the way you feel."

"Mac?" Addy said softly, wondering why his pacing had increased. "What are you trying to say?"

He dragged his hand through his hair. "You can't marry Parsnips." Mac exhaled a sigh of relief. Finally it was out. He rushed on, not daring to look at Addy. "I know things probably aren't very clear right now, and we've got a lot more to talk about, and to iron out, but in spite of all that, I just can't let you marry him."

"I know." Now that she had actually put it into words, Addy knew it was fact. She couldn't marry Pernall, not when she was in love with Mac.

"Now, you may have known him your whole life, but I don't think that amounts to a—" He glanced up at her. "Wh . . . what did you say?"

She smiled at him. She'd been wondering how long it would take him to realize she had spoken. "I said I'm not going to marry Pernall."

Mac stopped his pacing, coming to a halt directly in front of her. "When did you decide that?"

Addy shrugged. "Tonight. I realized when we were in Reno that it would be a mistake. It wouldn't be fair to him, or to me." She looked at Mac with eyes filled with love. "How can I marry another man when it's you I love?"

Mac grinned. "Oh, Addy." He reached out and drew her to her feet, holding her in his arms. "I love you, too." He held her for a few moments, wanting to be certain this was real and not a dream.

Addy allowed Mac to pull her closer, slipping her arms around his waist. Mac loved her. Her heart soared. All of her life she had wondered what it would feel like to have a man's love, but now she realized it wasn't just any man's love she wanted, but the *right* man's. And she knew without a doubt Mac was the right man. Love made all the difference in the world. And holding him in her arms, Addy knew this was right. This was how love was supposed to feel.

"Addy?" Mac drew back to look at her. "There are some things we have to talk about, but I want to know...if you'll marry me?" His face looked so expectant Addy laughed softly.

"Yes. Yes!" Her heart soared with love as Mac grabbed her around the waist and twirled her around.

Now that he knew she loved him, Mac hoped she would understand why he had done what he did. He prayed he could make her understand. He had to; he simply had to. He couldn't lose Addy, not now. Not ever. "I love you, Addy, and no matter what happens, I want you to remember that, promise?"

"I promise." But Addy knew nothing could happen, nothing could go wrong, not now, not when she was so happy. Addy frowned suddenly. Mac was right, there were some things they still had to take care of, like finding her grandfather and handling Pernall.

"Are you worried about Parsnips?" Mac asked, setting her back down on her feet, and knowing instantly by her reaction that he was right.

"Yes. And no."

Mac cocked his head and looked at her carefully. "Would you care to elaborate?"

"Mac, he's going to be furious with me for leaving without telling him."

Mac scowled. "Addy, wait a minute. You're a grown woman, you don't have to ask anyone's permission before you do something. This guy's not your father. You should have stopped taking orders from adults when you became one. He has no right to be angry, Addy. If anything, *you're* the one who should be angry after the way he treated your aunt. And Walter," he added. "Does Parsnips always behave like that?"

"Pernall's very...excitable," Addy explained lamely.

"Excitable," Mac said in derision. "I think he's a jerk. I don't know how you even could have considered marrying him."

"My reasons for considering his proposal were all wrong," Addy admitted. "I realize that now. *You made me realize that, Mac.* What you said about marrying a man for security really hit home. I was just going to marry Pernall because it's what my mother would have wanted. And," she added, taking a deep, trembling breath, "because I was afraid that was all life had to offer. But I realize now what you said was right." She grinned up at him. "For the first time in my life, I realize that my mother was wrong—about a lot of things. There is a lot more to life than Muncie and Pernall. Much more," she murmured, raising her face for Mac's kiss.

"I think we'd better talk," Mac said, unwinding his arms from around her and pulling her down on the couch next to him. "What are you going to say to him?" Mac asked, feeling an acute rush of jealousy.

"I don't know," Addy admitted, laying her head on Mac's shoulder. "I don't want to hurt him, Mac. And I know he's never going to be able to understand why I don't want to marry him. He's expected it since we were children." She sighed heavily. "Then there's the problem with Simpson House. I don't know how I'm going to get the money to pay the taxes, and if I don't, we'll lose the place." She glanced up at him and smiled. "You know, Mac, the thought of actually losing Simpson House doesn't bother me nearly as much as I thought it would. I realize now that home is where the heart is, and my heart is wherever you are." Mac gave her an affectionate squeeze. "And then, of course, there's still the matter of finding my grandfather." Addy shook her head. "Mac, honestly, where on earth could he be?"

Mac glanced away. He didn't want to talk to her about this tonight. He needed some time to think. He had to figure out the best way to handle this so she would understand, and right now he was feeling too happy and too content to spoil it.

"It's too late for you to worry about anything else tonight." He stood and drew her to her feet. "Right now, I think you should get some sleep. I think by tomorrow we should know where your grandfather is. He's bound to show up," Mac added, feeling guilty.

"Do you think so?" Addy asked hopefully, and Mac nodded.

"Don't worry," he ordered, leading her down the hall toward her bedroom. "Things will seem much clearer in the morning. I guarantee it. Now, go on and get some rest." He took her in his arms and kissed her very gently.

"Mac," she said, drawing back out of his arms. "I don't have any clothes. My suitcase is probably still at the airport and all my new clothes are still in Reno."

"I'll get you something. Wait right here." Mac was back with the top to a pair of his pajamas, grinning broadly. "This should fit."

Addy took it out of his hands and held it up in the air. "Your pajamas?" Chuckling softly, she hugged the top to her tightly. Somehow, wearing Mac's pajamas would make her feel close to him. "I love it, thanks," she said shyly.

"Good night, Addy," Mac said, planting a soft kiss on her lips.

"Good night, Mac." Clutching his pajamas close to her heart, Addy turned and went into the bedroom, shutting the door firmly behind her.

Mac wandered back into the living room, suddenly tired himself. He wasn't thrilled by the idea of Addy having to face Pernall. But she wouldn't have to do it alone. He'd be there with her. Mac intended to be there with her forever.

"Psst, Mac."

Startled, Mac jumped from his chair to find Blackie standing in the darkened kitchen doorway.

"Blackie!" Mac hissed, glancing around to be certain no one else in the house had heard him. "What the hell are you doing here? How did you get in?"

Blackie grinned impishly. "My little secret, son. My little secret." Blackie glanced around cautiously. "Is Addy in bed?"

Mac nodded and headed toward the kitchen. "What the hell are you doing here?" Mac pulled Blackie into the kitchen and out the back door into the moonlit night.

"I couldn't reach you on the phone," Blackie complained. "Something about an emergency at the casino."

Mac dragged a hand through his hair. What he didn't need tonight was another problem, and Blackie showing up at his house was definitely a problem.

"It's a long story. Myrtle's here—"

"Here! What's she doing *here*? Myrtle hates to fly!" Blackie stopped in his tracks, but Mac pulled him by the arm away from the house. The last thing he needed tonight was for Addy to discover him and her grandfather together. He'd never be able to explain that to her.

Mac nodded his head. "I know, but it's a long story. Parnsips showed up at Simpson House yesterday, and Myrtle told him Addy was here. He was pretty rough on her, and she got scared. She came to warn Addy that Pernall is on his way here to get her."

"Why, that little—"

"Never mind that now, Blackie, what are you doing *here*?" Mac asked, glancing back at the house and praying no one had heard their nocturnal visitor.

"There's something I think you should see."

Mac scowled. "Now?"

"Now." Blackie slid through the bushes to a waiting car. Mac followed and climbed in without question. If Blackie thought he should see something, then he'd better see it. Besides, he wanted to talk to him, and there was no time like the present.

They drove in silence to the casino and slipped in a back door. Blackie was quite specific with his feelings about not being seen. They headed to the privacy of Mac's office, where Blackie produced several videotapes, one of which he promptly inserted into Mac's machine.

"Now, I want you to watch this one carefully, Mac. Tell me what you see."

Mac watched in silence. He could tell by the layout that the tape was from the camera over one of the crap tables. Nothing looked unusual. The man who was shooting the dice looked ordinary enough, and the crew didn't look anything but bored.

"Do you notice anything special?" Blackie asked, perching on the corner of Mac's desk and absently rubbing his hip. It was an old war injury and was acting up, but not as much as usual. The dry Nevada weather helped a great deal.

Mac leaned forward in his chair. "The only thing I notice is that the guy shooting the dice doesn't know beans about how to throw dice. That's about the fifth time he's overshot the end of the table."

"Bingo," Blackie said, getting slowly to his feet. "You see, Mac, you've been searching for something really sophisticated, and with all your electronic equipment and gadgets, you've overlooked the obvious. Now take a look at this next tape." Blackie switched the tapes, then stood back to allow Mac to watch.

It was a shot of a blackjack table, a single-deck table, where the dealer dealt the cards by hand, as opposed to using what was known as a "shoe." When more than one deck was used in blackjack, the dealers dealt the cards from a plastic apparatus that held up to six decks of cards. It was done to prevent cheating more than anything else.

"Blackie," Mac complained. "I've been watching this thing for five minutes and I don't notice a thing out of sync."

"Precisely," Blackie said, snapping the machine off. "You see, Mac, you and your gadgets were looking for something out of sync, instead of looking for something out in the open; you know, like hide in plain sight. Let me explain. Let's start with the blackjack dealer. One deck, right, dealt by hand. Now, your sophisticated cameras can watch everything the dealer does. On the surface, it looks like she's doing nothing out of the ordinary. But up close, when you're sitting at the table, if you listen very, very carefully you'll hear a clicking sound."

Mac frowned. He didn't have the faintest idea what Blackie was talking about. "Clicking sound?"

"It's a sound that's made when a card is dealt from the bottom of the deck as opposed to the top of the deck like it's supposed to be. Usually, if the dealer's good, as this one is, you can't see the sleight of hand with the eye, or with your sophisticated gadgets." Blackie patted Mac on his shoulder. "You see, Mac, it's an old con, but a good one. The dealer has a shill sitting on the other side of the table as a player. He or she deals the card their partner needs to win, from the bottom of the deck. See, the dealer already knows what his hand is. So all the dealer has to do is make sure he buries the card his partner needs on the bottom, and then deals it to them. It's really quite simple. Then, at the end of the night, they split their winnings. Very elementary. Haven't seen this particular one for about twenty years. But it still works."

Mac was stunned. "What about the crap table? What's going on there?"

Blackie chuckled. "Now that's another oldie, but a goodie. But you see, because of all the sophisticated cameras, a con's got to have someone—usually the boxman, the man who sits at the table and is *supposed* to be in charge of the game—in on it. Now let's watch this tape again, but *really* watch it." Blackie snapped the machine back on and Mac leaned even closer. He watched the action carefully, but could not detect anything out of the ordinary, except that the man rolling the dice kept overshooting the end of the table.

"Blackie, I still don't see anything, except that the guy's overshooting the table."

"Precisely. Then what happens?" Blackie asked.

"You know what happens, Blackie, every time a pair of dice go off the table, they have to be inspected by the box-man to make sure they aren't loaded dice. Every day the dice are changed and numbered. All the boxman has to do is examine the dice and look for that day's number. As long as it matches, there's no problem."

"Wrong," Blackie said. "That's exactly the problem in this case. You see, every time the dice went off the table and were handed to the boxman who is in on this con, he exchanged the real dice for a loaded pair. He then handed them back to the shooter, who was his accomplice in this case. The man continued to roll, and then when he felt he had made enough numbers, and money, he rolled the dice off the table again, and then the boxman just went ahead and exchanged the loaded dice for the regular ones to pass on to the next shooter. It's quite simple, really. In my day, they used to sell loaded dice in sets of nine. Three pair were weighted toward the high numbers, three for the low, and the other three were perfectly normal. I suspect they're using something similar."

Mac reached out and turned off the machine, shaking his head in awe. "Blackie, how on earth did you ever discover this?" Mac was genuinely impressed.

Blackie smiled, his eyes twinkling. "That, my boy, is my little secret."

"How many people do you think are involved?" Mac asked, already trying to calculate how this could hurt the casino.

"I *know* there are five. The boxman, the blackjack dealer, two shills from that table and the dice shooter."

Mac sighed and ran a hand through his hair. "How many employees?" His stomach tensed as he waited for Blackie's response.

"Only two. The dealer and the boxman. That's why I needed to check the personnel records. I wasn't sure if this was an amateur, or a full-scale ring. If you'll check, you'll see that although the boxman and the dealer have different names, they're married. The boxman's been working here at the Parkland for a couple of years. The dealer was just hired about six months ago. I suspect they've had this planned for a while, and I also suspect they've played this game with more than one casino."

"I'm going to have to fire them," Mac announced grimly, relieved that the problem was not as widespread as he had feared.

"Not necessary," Blackie said with a smile, pulling a wad of money out of his pocket. "Had a nice little chat with them this afternoon. Seems they found it necessary to resign, and thought it best that they turn this over to you."

Mac stared in shock at the money Blackie held out to him. He couldn't believe it. "How on earth did you get them—"

"Like I said, my boy, it's my little secret. Now, I do believe you and I have some business to conclude."

"Gladly," Mac announced with a smile, counting one-half of the money and handing it over to Blackie as promised. It amounted to quite a tidy sum, but Mac would have gladly paid triple the price just to have this over with. "Now, Blackie, there's something else we need to discuss."

"Addy?" Blackie asked with a knowing smile. He nodded his head. "I thought so."

"Blackie, listen to me. I realize I haven't known Addy very long, but I don't think that's very important. It's not the length of time—"

"Son, son, son." Blackie held up his hand. "Are you trying to tell me you love my granddaughter?"

Mac smiled. "Yes, I guess I am."

Blackie grinned, thoroughly pleased at the prospect. "Then what's the problem?"

"What's the problem?" Mac growled. "Blackie, do you realize you and I, the two men Addy supposedly trusts most in the world, have been lying to her and deceiving her? How do you think she's going to feel when she finds that out?"

Blackie absently scratched his chin. "Yes, mmm, well, I think you might have a point, there, MacArthur. Got any suggestions?"

Mac knew he had to approach this carefully. "Blackie, I know you never wanted Addy to know about your past, but she's not her mother. She loves you, you're the most important person in her life. I think you've underestimated her, and her reactions."

"Are you suggesting I tell her the truth?" Blackie asked dubiously, not liking the trend of this conversation.

"I'm suggesting we *both* tell her the truth. About everything. Blackie, we both love her, and I think it's about time that we come clean with her and tell everything."

"Don't you think we're taking a bit of a risk?" Blackie asked.

"Of course, but that's the price we're going to have to pay. I love her, Blackie, and I've asked her to marry me. But I want to come clean with her, and I can't and won't do that without your permission. How can we start off marriage with lies and deceptions between us? If we do, when Addy finds out the truth—and she will, eventually—she'll never be able to trust me. That's no way to start a relationship. What I've done is bad enough already. But I gave you my word that I wouldn't reveal any part of our agreement to anyone. You held up your end of the bargain, and I *have* to hold up mine. But I don't have to like it, and I don't.''

Blackie cocked his head and looked at Mac carefully. ''You've got a point, son, and character. I like that.'' Blackie grinned. ''I would be pleased and proud to have you as my grandson, even if it is through marriage. And as for the other, maybe you're right. Maybe it's about time I tell Addy the truth. Like you say, if she loves me, it shouldn't matter. And if I know my Addy, it won't. Probably should have told her years ago, but I guess I was just chicken. But if you've got the guts to tell her the truth, then I'd better have, too. That child means the world to me, Mac, and I wouldn't want anything to hurt her.''

''And neither would I,'' Mac said firmly, relieved that finally he was going to be able to be truthful with Addy. It would be a new beginning for them. He suddenly couldn't wait to tell her, to see her beautiful face, to let her know how he felt.

''Blackie, I want to take care of this as soon as possible. But I think we should do this together. Come by the house in the morning, around nine. I'll talk to her a bit beforehand.''

Blackie nodded, glancing hurriedly at his watch. ''I hate to rush you, Mac, but I've got to get a move on. I borrowed that car and I've got to get it back.'' Blackie grinned. ''Before the owner discovers I've borrowed it.'' With a wink, Blackie was gone.

''Nine o'clock,'' Mac called as Blackie disappeared around the corner. Mac smiled, and sank down onto a chair.

By tomorrow morning, everything would be settled, and finally Addy would be his. Another thought caused him to groan. What did Blackie mean he had to get the car back before the owner realized he had borrowed it? Chuckling softly, Mac stood up, shut down the lights and locked his office. The first thing he was going to have to do after he and Addy were married was to get Blackie some line of work—something that could put his legitimate talents to use. It was a shame to let them go to waste. He'd been thinking about looking over a new land site in Laughlin, Nevada. It would be a perfect place to build a new Parkland casino. But with just him and Rosie, they didn't have enough manpower to start another casino without some help, help they could trust. An idea began forming slowly in his mind. Mac yawned and rubbed his eyes wearily. It had been a long day, and he had too much on his mind right now to explore the idea any further. There would be plenty of time for that later. Right now, he had to handle the most pressing problem. Addy.

He couldn't wait until tomorrow, when this charade would finally, and blessedly, be over. And Addy would be his. Forever.

Chapter Nine

The jangling of the bell kept ringing, but Mac rolled over in bed and tried to ignore it. "It can't be morning already," he groaned, blindly reaching out to shut off his alarm. But it wasn't his alarm, he realized. Whatever bell was ringing kept on ringing.

It had been almost two by the time he had gotten back to the house. Mac had crept in silently and nearly had been startled to death to find Hildy and her spoon waiting for him in the darkened kitchen. She'd thought he was a burglar and had gotten in a good swipe before he convinced her he belonged there.

There was no easy explanation as to what he was doing creeping into the house in the middle of the night, never mind what a strange woman and a pigeon were doing in her house. She'd made a pot of coffee as Mac poured out the tale, promising her that first thing in the morning Blackie would be arriving and they were going to tell Addy the truth.

Blackie! Mac bolted upright in bed. That must be Blackie ringing the doorbell. Jumping out of bed, Mac grabbed a pair of jeans and fussed with the zipper before running barefoot to the front door. He yanked it open, and his sleepy eyes widened as they landed on the pair of gentlemen standing there. One was Blackie, all right, but he wasn't alone. There was another man with him, a smaller man who reminded Mac of a fireplug. He was short and squatty; his chest was as wide as his legs. He reminded Mac of a disproportioned dachshund. Judging from the scowl on his face, Mac had an idea he had just laid eyes on the infamous Pernall Ditkus.

"Where is she?" the man demanded, taking Blackie by the arm and dragging him through the doorway.

"Sorry, Mac," Blackie said sheepishly, shaking free. "I guess I got a bit carried away. Pernall here found me at the blackjack table this morning. Just trying my hand," he assured Mac as he started to scowl.

"Where is Adeline?" Pernall demanded, glancing around the house.

"She's sleeping," Mac replied sourly, crossing his arms against his bare chest. "Not that it's any of your business."

"None of my business!" Pernall drew back, looking positively disgusted. "I'll have you know, good man—"

"Lower your voice," Mac ordered, getting a little disgusted himself. "Before you wake up the whole house."

"I'm already awake, Mac," Addy said, walking into the room and rubbing her eyes sleepily.

"Adeline!" At the sound of Pernall's voice, Addy froze. Her eyes sprung open, and she looked from her grandfather to Pernall, not certain who she was more surprised to see.

"Grandpa!" she cried, flying into his arms. Addy hugged him tight. She had never been so happy to see anyone in her life. She cast Mac a happy glance over her shoulder. He had been right all along. He had said he'd help her find her grandfather. She drew back and looked at her grandfather reproachfully. "Where on earth have you been?" she scolded. "Mac and I have been looking all over for you." Addy missed the glances Mac and Blackie exchanged.

"Around," Blackie said mysteriously, giving Pernall a smug look.

"Adeline." Pernall's voice was low and controlled. "May I ask what on earth is going on? And what is that that you have on?" His fuzzy brows drew together in a frown as they roamed over Mac's pajama top, which barely skimmed the top of her thighs, leaving the rest of her long legs bare. He drew himself up, his face cold. "That's hardly what I consider proper attire for my bride-to-be." His gaze moved to Mac, who was doing a little scowling of his own. Pernall was obviously displeased by his attire, as well. "And who may I ask is *this*?"

"This," Addy said, lifting her chin defiantly, "is MacArthur Cole. He's been helping me look for my grandfather." Once again Blackie and Mac exchanged silent glances.

"Is that what they've been telling you?" Pernall laughed. "Well, Adeline, I can see it's a good thing I arrived when I did," he announced smugly. "When I couldn't locate you yesterday afternoon, I did some checking. It only confirmed what I had learned previously. Do you remember when you applied to me for a mortgage to save Simpson House?" He didn't give her a chance to answer. "Well, I did a little background checking on your grandfather, and—"

"You checked up on my grandfather?" Addy was appalled. When Pernall had refused them a mortgage, he had told her it was purely business, that they were a poor credit risk. She had tried not to be offended, but she was. She couldn't understand why Pernall couldn't make an exception in this case; after all, he had known her his whole life. It wasn't as if she were a stranger walking in off the street. That alone should have given her an indication of Pernall's true personality.

"Well, certainly I checked up on him, and you should be thankful I did. I thought it was very interesting that no one had ever heard of the man before he arrived in Muncie. I had the best private investigators on the case for the past few months, and I think you'd be very interested in learning what I found out about your precious grandfather." He gave Blackie a scathing look, unaware of the dangerous glint of anger in Addy's eyes.

"You put a detective on my grandfather? How dare you!" she fumed, taking a step closer to him until they were toe to toe. "How dare you do such a thing." The man had gone too far this time. First he had scared her aunt, now he was prying into her grandfather's personal life. "What right do you have to pry into my grandfather's background or personal life?"

"Every right in the world," Pernall said confidently, glancing at Blackie in disdain. "You have to remember, as my wife-to-be, I had every right to know *everything* about you. *And* your family. I have my family name to think of, Adeline, I mean, let's be reasonable."

His words caused Addy's temper to blow. He sounded like her mother, more concerned with a family name and legacy than with people's feelings. How on earth could she have ever even have considered spending her life with this man?

"I don't care what the reasons were, Pernall. I'm disgusted that you would stoop to such levels. If you wanted to know something, you should have come right out and asked me, or my grandfather. I'm sure he would have told you anything you wanted to know. I'm appalled at your behavior.''

"Well, you won't be so appalled when you find out just exactly what I learned. And as for your grandfather telling me anything I wanted to know, I seriously doubt it, Adeline. He can't even tell *you* the truth, so what makes you think he'd be any more honest with me?''

"Are you calling my grandfather a liar?'' Sparks of anger darkened her eyes, and Addy balled her hands into fists as fury rolled over her delicate frame. Her grandfather was one of the most important people in her life, and she wasn't about to let anyone talk about him this way, especially not Pernall.

"Liar?'' Pernall laughed. "I'd say that was putting it mildly. I think you should know that I also did some checking on this . . . this . . .'' He glanced at Mac with a look of disgust. "MacArthur character.''

"Mac is not a character,'' Addy said hotly. She glared at Pernall reproachfully. "Mac's been wonderful to me. I don't know what I would have done without him.''

Shaking his head in amusement, Pernall laughed softly. "Addy, you are the most naive person I've ever met. It's a good thing I came when I did. Don't you know what's been going on? Don't you know what these two have been doing to you?'' He shook his head. "I can see that I'm going to have to really keep an eye on you after we're married. Your judgment obviously can't be trusted.''

"Pernall,'' Mac warned, his voice low and controlled. "You'd better watch it.'' He wasn't about to stand here and let this idiot insult Adeline. There was a limit to his patience, and Pernall had just about reached it.

"Addy,'' Mac said, dropping his arm around her shoulder and pulling her away from Pernall. He didn't like the direction Pernall's conversation was taking. He wanted a chance to explain things to Addy in his own way, and he certainly didn't need Parsnips's help. "There are some things you and I and your grandfather need to talk about." He glanced at Pernall. *"Alone."*

"Take your hands off of her," Pernall ordered, clearly not seeing the peril he was in. "I won't have my bride-to-be manhandled."

Mac's jaw tightened. "The only thing that's going to be manhandled around here is *you*, if you don't shut your mouth."

"What's the matter?" Pernall suddenly demanded, a sly smile on his face. "Afraid I'll tell Addy the truth about what's been going on? Afraid I'll tell her how her precious grandfather has been lying to her all these years and how you've been playing her for a fool? Oh, yes, I know all about you and Mr. La Rue." Pernall glanced at Blackie. "Your dirty little secret isn't quite a secret anymore."

Mac took a step closer to Pernall, fully determined to make the man a few inches shorter in the swiftest amount of time, but Addy grabbed his arm and held him back. Addy looked from her grandfather to Mac in confusion. Her face clouded with uneasiness as she struggled to understand what was going on. "What is he talking about?" she asked, looking first at Mac, then her grandfather. "What dirty little secret? I don't understand." Neither man answered; they both glanced away. With her uneasiness growing, Addy turned on Pernall.

"I want to know what on earth you are talking about, right now!"

Pernall leaned back on his heels and crossed his arms against his chest. "As I was saying, I've done my homework. You'd be surprised how loose some lips become when they see the color of money. As I've suspected all along, your grandfather's not the kindly old retired gentleman he pretends to be.''

Her spirits nosedived as neither her grandfather nor Mac stepped forward to dispute Pernall's claims. ''I think you'd better explain yourself,'' she whispered.

''It seems that your grandfather was quite notorious, in his day—''

''In my day,'' Blackie huffed, clearly insulted. ''Listen, you little whippersnapper, I've a good mind—''

''Grandpa,'' Addy said sternly. ''Let Pernall finish.''

''It seems your grandfather was one of the best con men in the business. He was so good, in fact, people around these parts still talk about him. That's how I found out so much about him.'' He glanced at the older man scornfully. ''They called him Blackie. He and Mac's grandfather were the most famous con men in the history of Las Vegas. That's how Mac got his casino. His grandfather and your grandfather *cheated* people.'' His voice rose an octave in his excitement. ''Oh, they were clever about it, very clever, they were never arrested or convicted of anything, but all the same, they were nothing but common criminals.''

''I don't believe you,'' Addy stammered. She turned to her grandfather. ''Is it true?'' she whispered. ''Is it?''

Blackie nodded. ''But it's not the way this... this... bushwhacker makes it sound.'' Blackie drew himself up and looked down his nose at Pernall. His blue eyes sparkled with anger. ''We were *not* criminals, and we were certainly anything but *common*.'' Blackie sniffed. ''Not that I'd expect the likes of you to understand.''

''Why?'' Addy stared at her grandfather in confusion. ''Why didn't you just tell me the truth? All these years...'' Her voice trailed off. Suddenly things began to make sense. Now she understood why her mother had turned her back on Blackie. Now she understood why her mother had been so ashamed of her own father. But didn't Grandpa know she wasn't her mother? She wasn't anything like her mother. But maybe her grandfather didn't know that. Her whole life, she had been trying to live the way her mother would have wanted her to, and maybe her grandfather feared that if she knew the truth, she too would feel about him the way her mother had. Dear Lord. Didn't Grandpa know that there wasn't a thing in this world that could ever make her stop loving him? "Grandpa," she began softly. "You should have just told me the truth a long time ago. *I love you.* I'm not my mother, I'm *me*, and whatever you've done, no matter what it is, I love you. I'll always love you."

Ignoring Pernall's startled gasps, Addy went to her grandfather and wrapped her arms around his neck.

"Oh, Addy," Blackie said, hugging her tight. "I wanted to tell you lots of times, but I was so afraid you'd be ashamed of me—like your mother. I lost your mother because of what I had done, and I couldn't bear to lose you. You're the most important thing in my life."

"Grandpa," Addy said softly, drawing back to look at him. "I could never be ashamed of you. I can't change what my mother did—or was—but I'm *nothing* like her. I know that now." She glanced warmly at Mac. "I feel a little bad that you didn't trust me enough to tell me the truth, but I can understand why you didn't. But from now on, no more secrets. All right?"

Blackie nodded, much to Pernall's chagrin. "I don't believe this," he huffed. "How on earth can you simply dismiss what your grandfather's done! Adeline, your grandfather has been *lying* to you your whole life. Doesn't that mean anything to you?"

Addy turned in her grandfather's arms. "Yes, Pernall, it means that my grandfather loved me and was afraid to hurt me." She smiled at him. "It means that he cared enough

about me and my feelings not to want to risk hurting me."
That was more than she could say for Pernall. He had no
right to reveal this information to her. This was something
her grandfather should have been allowed to tell her in his
own time, in his own way. What Pernall had done was un-
forgivable.

"Oh, for heaven's sake," Pernall said. "Addy, you are
the most simpleminded—"

"That's enough," Mac interrupted.

Pernall whirled on Mac. "And as for you, what's your
excuse for lying to Addy?" His words hung heavy in the air.
Addy slowly turned toward Mac.

"Mac?"

"Addy." Mac shifted uncomfortably. He had a feeling
she wouldn't be quite as forgiving toward him as she'd been
toward her grandfather—not unless he had a chance to explain—in his own way. "Please, let me explain."

"Yes. Do." Pernall gloated. "I'd like to hear just how
you can explain to Addy that while you were supposed to be
helping her find her grandfather, what you were in fact
doing was preventing her from finding him. Isn't that
right?" Pernall challenged. "Haven't you spent the last few
days entertaining Addy so that her grandfather could prac-
tice his illegal activities without her knowing?"

Addy turned to Mac, her heart numb. Entertaining her?
Is that all this had meant to Mac? Was what Pernall said
true? Addy felt a cloud of pain blur her vision. "Is that
true?" she whispered, feeling her heart slowly shattering.
Oh, God. "Is it true?"

"Addy, please," Mac pleaded. "Let me explain." The
urge to send Pernall back to Muncie—without a plane—was
so strong Mac could hardly contain himself. He reached for
her, but she shrank away from him. He couldn't bear to see
the pain in her eyes. He had vowed no one would ever hurt

Addy again, and he had unwittingly been the culprit. "You *have* to listen to my side. It's not the way he makes it sound."

"Addy." Her grandfather brushed Pernall aside to get to her. He'd never seen her looking so pale, so fragile, so vulnerable. His heart ached for what his deceptions had cost Addy. This was all his fault. Had he been truthful with her right from the beginning, none of this would have happened. Blackie took her in his arms. "Honey, please, don't listen to this...bushwhacker. He doesn't know what he's talking about. Listen to Mac. Hear him out. This is all my fault. Mac was doing me a favor, that's all—"

"Oh, shut up," Pernall ordered. "I think she's heard more than enough from the *both* of you."

Addy's eyes were locked on Mac's. She couldn't hear or see anything but him. This couldn't be happening. How could Mac have done such a thing? Why would he lie to her? *She believed him.* He had asked her to trust him and she had. Oh, what a fool she'd been.

"Addy, please hear my side," Mac pleaded, but she shook her head.

"No." Her voice was barely a whisper and she held up her hand. "Don't say anything. Please. Not another word. You've said enough. Done enough." Her voice broke.

"And that's not half of it," Pernall went on, oblivious to the tension filling the room.

"Oh, God," Addy whimpered. She couldn't bear to hear any more. She turned, fully intending to flee, but Pernall caught her arm and stopped her.

"Where are you going? I'm not finished yet." He frowned at her. "And why are you crying? I certainly hope you haven't done anything to disgrace yourself." He glanced at Mac. "Particularly with this...this...*gambler*. We do have the family name to think of."

"Who you calling a *gambler*?" Hildy roared, storming into the room and brandishing her wooden spoon right in Pernall's line of vision. Obviously she'd been eavesdropping from the kitchen.

"Not another crazy woman!" Pernall cried, jumping back out of range of Hildy's swinging arm. "First, that old fool with the pigeon, and now this one. Honestly, Addy, what do you do to attract them?"

"Oh, God," Addy whimpered, unable to stop the tears from falling. She had to get away from here, away from everything and everyone. With a barely concealed sob, Addy turned and fled through the kitchen doors. She could hear Mac and her grandfather calling her. She could hear the commotion going on in the living room, but she couldn't stop. She just kept going, wanting only to stop the unbearable pain that pulsated through her body.

The sight of Addy's anguish caused something to snap inside of Mac. He grabbed Pernall by the front of his shirt and hoisted him right off his feet. "Get out of my house," he growled, his voice low and dangerous. "Now. Before I throw you out."

Pernall swallowed hard several times. His feet dangled in the air as he tried valiantly to get loose of Mac. "N-not until I get my bride-to-be."

Mac shook his head. "You don't know when to leave well enough alone, do you? First you go around scaring harmless old women, now you think you can come into my home, insult my family and start calling the shots. Who the hell do you think you are?"

"Shots? Shots! Did someone say shots?" Myrtle toddled into the living room with Walter perched on her arm. The moment Walter set eyes on Pernall, he let out a piercing screech, fluttered his wings and dove directly toward Pernall, pecking at his balding pate.

"Get him off," Pernall screamed amidst Walter's screeching. Myrtle screamed as Pernall swung at Walter.

"Blackie, Mac, please, do something," Myrtle cried, wringing her hands in dismay as Walter continued shrieking and Pernall continued swinging. "He's going to hurt poor Walter. Oh, please, do something!"

Blackie and Mac exchanged smiles. "Gladly."

"Let me," Blackie insisted, lifting his fist and connecting it with Pernall's pointy little nose. The man went sprawling to the floor, holding his nose.

"You idiot," Pernall cried, scooting backward. "Look what you've done." Pernall looked at his hand, his eyes wide and wild. "I'm bleeding!" He scrambled to his feet. "I'm going to sue you, all of you."

Hildy stepped forward as Walter flew back to the safety of Myrtle's arm. "Well, as long as you're going to sue someone, you might as well add me to the list." Hildy lifted her spoon in the air. Pernall reared back, then turned and fled with Hildy hot on his heels, brandishing the spoon at his retreating back.

"My poor baby," Myrtle cooed, petting Walter. "You're so distressed." She bent to kiss the bird's beak. "That nasty little man. You won't have to worry about him any longer. Will we?" she asked Mac hopefully.

Mac smiled and gently touched Myrtle's cheek. "No, you won't have to worry about him anymore."

Beaming, Myrtle reached up and kissed Mac's cheek. "Come on, sweetie," she said, turning her attention to Walter. "I'll put you back to bed so you can rest." Myrtle drifted back into her bedroom, leaving Mac and Blackie alone.

"What am I going to do?" Mac asked.

"Do? Well, son, do you love her?"

Mac nodded. "Of course I do, you know that."

"Then are you going to let her go without a fight?"

"No."

"Didn't think so." Blackie smiled as Hildy stomped back into the house, muttering under her breath and holding her broken spoon in her hand.

"What happened here?" she asked as Mac pushed by her in a hurry.

"Nothing," Blackie said, glancing over Hildy's shoulder at her broken spoon. "What happened to you?"

"Nothing," she snapped, giving as much information as she'd been given. Ignoring Blackie, she marched into the kitchen, trying to find some glue to repair her spoon. Blackie peered over her shoulder, drawing her ire.

"Get back," she yelled. "You're in my light. Can't you see when a body's busy? Damn fool caused me to break my spoon."

"I'll buy you another," Blackie offered. "If you'll make me some breakfast."

"I can buy my own spoons," Hildy huffed, smiling in spite of herself. "And you can make your own breakfast. Pigeons in my bedrooms and fighting in my living room. What's this world coming to?" She glanced at Blackie through narrowed eyes. "All this commotion wouldn't have something to do with you, would it?" One silver brow lifted and she nodded her head. "Humph, I thought so."

"So how about it, do I get some breakfast?"

"No!"

"Hildy," Blackie teased, coming up behind her. "You're such a charmer." He patted her gently on the bottom. "I'll bet you tell that to all the men."

"You want breakfast?"

"Yes."

"Then get out of my kitchen," she ordered, totally unnerved by the man's presence. "Don't like anyone in my kitchen when I'm cooking. Gives me hives. If you want something to eat you're going to have to skedaddle."

"Skedaddle, huh?" Blackie smiled, and grabbed an apron off a hook near the door. "Come on, Hildy," he coaxed, sidling up behind her and talking very softly. "*I'll* give you a hand," he offered, winking at her as she turned to look at him. "Besides, what's a little hives between friends?"

Chapter Ten

Addy was sitting by the pool, hugging her knees. Mac stood silently for a moment just watching her, his heart aching for the pain he had caused her. "Addy? Can we talk?"

She didn't turn and she didn't speak, but he could tell by the trembling in her shoulders that she was crying. He went to her and sat down on the edge of the same chair. He wanted to haul her into his arms and kiss away her tears. But he couldn't. Not yet. He had to talk to her. He had to explain.

"Addy, I know you're very upset right now, but I want to tell you something. Do you remember last night, when I told you there were some things I wanted to tell you? But we never got the chance because Aunt Myrtle showed up." He waited for a response. When none was forthcoming, Mac continued. "Anyway, what I wanted to tell you was the truth. Believe me, I didn't like lying to you any more than you liked it, but I had no choice. I'd made a promise to

Blackie, a promise I couldn't break, but that was *before* I had even met you.

"From the moment you walked into my office, I knew there was something special about you. I will admit I lied to you about helping you find your grandfather—"

She turned to look at him, and his heart constricted. Her eyes were red, her face tearstained. His arms ached for her, but he knew he couldn't reach for her yet.

"But at least let me explain. Someone was stealing money from the casino. Rosie and I couldn't figure it out. That's when I turned to your grandfather. I called him and told him that if he could learn the identity of the culprit, I would give him half of all the money that the casino had lost. He agreed. I didn't know *why* he agreed, but I later learned it was to earn the money to pay the taxes on Simpson House."

She lifted her head and looked at Mac, suddenly understanding a bit. "That's what this was all about?"

Mac nodded. At least she was listening to him, at least it was a beginning. "Your grandfather had only two stipulations: I had to let him work in his own way, and I couldn't tell *anyone* he was back in town or back in business. I agreed, but that was *before* you showed up in my office. Neither one of us expected it, in fact I didn't even know about you until the moment I laid eyes on you." Mac reached out and took her trembling hand in his. "But I had already made a promise to Blackie, and I couldn't go back on my word.

"Anyway, when I told Blackie you were here, and that you were looking for him to tell him you were going to marry Parsnips in order to save Simpson House, well, Blackie got mighty upset."

Addy smiled tentatively. She could just imagine what her grandfather had to say about that.

"Anyway, when Blackie heard that, he said it was more important than ever that he find the culprit victimizing the casino *before* you went back home. He was afraid if you went home, you'd marry Parsnips. So, he made me promise that I'd keep you here long enough for him to solve the casino caper.

"The way he figured it, if I kept you here, we'd *all* get what we wanted. I'd get the culprit, you'd have the money to save Simpson House, and Blackie wouldn't have to watch his only granddaughter marry Parsnips."

His words caused her to smile. Hopeful, Mac went on. "Now I went along with your grandfather, Addy, because I'd given him my word and I'm a man of my word, even though it meant I had to lie to you. I admit it, and I'm sorry. But that's the *only* thing I lied to you about." He looked down at her gently. "I meant every word I said about us. I love you, Addy, and I still want to marry you—if you'll have me?"

Addy looked at Mac, her eyes shining with love. It was either now or never. She had to make a decision. Love and Mac were here, waiting for her. Addy realized she deserved to love and be loved. Life was meant to be savored and enjoyed. All she had to do was reach out and grab it with both hands. It meant finally burying the past and starting anew—with Mac by her side.

Despite everything that had happened, she loved Mac more than anything in the world. His intentions had been honorable, his methods had just gone askew. But he did love her, of that she had no doubt. She could see it in his eyes, hear it in his voice, read it in his smile.

Laughing, she threw her arms around him and hugged him tight. "Yes, yes, I'll marry you."

"Oh, Addy." Mac's lips found hers. Tremors of delight skipped up and down her frame as her pulse began to pound. His lips worked over hers, gently at first, then more urgently.

With a sigh, Mac drew away from her. "Oh, Addy," he whispered, holding her close. "It's a good thing there's no waiting time to get married in this state. I've waited long enough. I want my ring on your finger before you change your mind."

Addy laughed softly. "I'm not going to change my mind," she assured him.

"Good." He pulled her to her feet. "Then let's go."

"Go? Go where? Mac," she protested, trying to stop him. "I'm not even dressed. For that matter, I don't even have any clothes, if you remember."

"No clothes, huh?" He did his best not to leer at her, but couldn't help himself. A flush raced across her cheeks at his teasing expression. He touched her face tenderly. "I hope you always blush, Addy. I love it. And you do have clothes—at least one dress, the white one. James sent it down by car this morning."

"Oh, Mac."

He grinned and grabbed her hand as they walked. "I told you I had something special planned for that dress."

"Mac?" Addy frowned. "I think we've got a few things to settle first, don't we?"

"Like what? The most important things are already worked out. You love me. I love you. What else is there?"

"Mac, what am I going to do about Simpson House, and Grandpa, and Aunt Myrtle?" Addy sighed heavily, leaning against Mac. "And let's not forget about Walter."

"I've already got that all figured out. As for your grandfather, I'm going to offer him a position as a security consultant for the Parkland. It's about time we put all his vast . . . experience to work. And as for your aunt and Walter . . . I've got an idea." Arm in arm they walked around the pool and toward the back of Mac's property. "You see all this," he said, sweeping his arm across the landscape. "It's Cole land for as far as the eye can see. Nevada has the perfect year-round climate for retirees, and it's much cheaper to live here than anywhere else because we have no state taxes, and expenses are so reasonable because of all the revenue brought in from gambling. I was thinking we could build a little home on the back of the property." He looked down at her. "I figured you and I can keep the main house, and we can build a smaller one in back for Rosie and Aunt Myrtle. So, what do you think?"

She hugged him tightly. "I think it's a wonderful idea. But how is Rosie going to feel about sharing her home with Aunt Myrtle and a pigeon?"

Mac chuckled softly. "Addy, wait until you meet Rosie. She's wonderful, and she's absolutely dotty about animals—any kind. And as for your aunt, how could anyone not love her?"

"Oh, Mac," Addy whispered, overcome with love for him. "But there's still the problem of selling Simpson House."

"You know, you don't have to sell it, hon. I'm sure we can hire someone competent to run it."

Addy shook her head. It was time to let go of the past and the pain, and time to go forward into the future. A future filled with love and happiness. "No, Mac, I think it's best. My home is wherever you are."

Mac hugged her tightly. "Oh, Addy, we're going to have such a wonderful life. I'm going to take you places, we're going to see things and do things." Mac began planning quickly. "What would you think about an African safari for our honeymoon? Rosie will be back in a few weeks and I can take some time off. I think a month or so should do it. What do you think?'' They started walking back toward the house, their arms wrapped around each other.

"Africa?" Addy croaked. "That depends."

"On what?" Mac asked with a frown.

"On if we can get there by train."

Chuckling, Mac scooped Addy up in his arms. "You're not still afraid of flying, are you?"

"Petrified."

"How do you feel about swimming?"

"Swimming?" Addy asked cautiously as Mac circled around the pool. "Mac. *MacArthur*," she screeched a moment before he jumped into the pool, dunking them both. Sputtering, Addy's arms sought his in the cool water.

Mac hauled her close. "I told you, Addy, we're going to do things and see things you've only dreamed about."

Addy pushed a wadded mass of hair off her face. "Getting dunked in a cold pool while I'm practically naked is not something I've dreamed about," she complained good-humoredly. "This is more like a nightmare."

"Every day for the rest of our lives is going to be an adventure, Addy. I love you," Mac said between kisses. "*I love you*. Do you know how happy you've made me?"

"And you," she scolded, "do you know how wet you've made me?" Laughing, she pushed his head under the water and swam like a fish toward the side of the pool. Climbing the ladder, Addy looked down at Mac. Yes, her mother had been wrong, very wrong. But it suddenly didn't matter anymore. She had finally found the courage to reach out for love. She had dared to want more instead of settling for less. Mac climbed out of the pool, and together they walked toward the house.

Addy's spirits were high, her heart soaring. She finally knew who she was and where she was going. But more importantly she knew that no matter what, she would have Mac and his love with her every step of the way.

She had only wanted one precious, treasured memory. Instead, she had dared to dream, and now she had found a *lifetime* of memories and a lifetime of love.

Addy looked up at Mac. What more could a woman ask for?

Epilogue

The moment Mac saw her standing in his office, he knew there was trouble. "Addy?"

She whirled to face him, her expression a worried frown. "Oh, Mac," she breathed, instinctively going into his arms for comfort.

"Shh, it's all right, hon. What's wrong?"

She sighed heavily and pulled back to look at him. "Mac, you're not going to believe what's happened."

Mac smiled. "Walter got loose again?"

She shook her head. "Worse," she said glumly.

"Aunt Myrtle's been playing the slot machines again?"

She shook her head. "Wrong, again."

He grinned. "Hildy broke her wooden spoon?" he asked hopefully, and she shook her head.

Mac frowned. "Honey, I'm running out of answers." He scratched his head, suddenly nervous. "This wouldn't have anything to do with you and I, does it?" he asked worriedly. "We've only been back from Africa for three days. Don't tell me the honeymoon is over already?"

Addy laughed softly, hugging him tight. As far as she was concerned, the honeymoon was never going to be over.

"Out with it, then," he ordered, knowing whatever was troubling her had to be important. They had cut their three-month trip short by a week because Addy hadn't been feeling well. "Addy?" His face grew ashen and he clutched her shoulders. "You're not sick, are you?"

"Sick? No." She shook her head. "Mac, he's done it again."

Mac frowned. "Who's done what again?"

"Grandpa," she said with a heavy sigh. "He's disappeared again."

Mac groaned softly. Blackie had promised to behave while they were on their honeymoon, but evidently since they were back now, he felt no compulsion to keep his promise.

"Now where did he go?" Mac asked, knowing Addy was going to be worried to death until they found him.

"I don't have the faintest idea. This morning when I got up, I walked over to the retirement home. It took me a while to get Walter to spill the beans, but he finally admitted Grandpa had slipped out in the middle of the night. Most of his clothes are still here, so I'm assuming he's coming back. When, I don't know."

"Don't worry, honey. I'm sure everything's all right. Let me call Rosie and have her look into it." Addy sat down in a chair opposite Mac's desk while he made several phone calls.

Fifteen minutes later, he hung up the receiver, grinning broadly. "Rosie found him!" he announced triumphantly.

"She did?" Addy jumped to her feet. "Now where is he?"

Mac came around his desk and drew Addy into his arms. "He's in Reno, Addy."

"Reno?" She frowned. "What on earth is he doing there? And why the heck didn't he just tell us he was going? Why all the secrecy?"

Mac chuckled sheepishly, rubbing his chin. "Maybe because he's not exactly... alone."

Addy looked at him suspiciously. This wasn't making any sense. "Mac, you've been hanging around Aunt Myrtle too long. What do you mean he's not exactly alone?"

Mac leaned forward and kissed her on the nose. "It seems Robert La Rue and Hildeguard Mentiant applied for a marriage certificate just a few hours ago. I guess your grandfather and Hildy have eloped."

"Eloped!" Stunned, Addy started to laugh. "I don't believe it. Hildy and Grandpa are getting married? Why didn't he just tell me?"

Mac shrugged his shoulders and glanced at his watch. "It's only an hour away, Addy. I can call Chip and tell him to get the plane ready. If we hurry we might just—what's the matter, Addy?" He went down on one knee as she sank into the chair. Her face had turned a peculiar shade of green. "Addy, don't tell me after flying all the way to Africa, you're going to get squeamish over a short flight to Reno?"

She shook her head, trying to calm her stomach. "The doctor said I shouldn't fly... for a while."

"Doctor! Doctor? Addy, my God, you didn't tell me you went to see a doctor. When? How? What's wrong? What did he say?"

Addy started laughing. She had never seen Mac so upset. It took a lot to rattle the man, but he was certainly rattled now. "Honey," she said calmly, placing a hand on his shoulder. "Relax. I'm fine."

"People who are fine don't go to doctors." His face creased in worry. "Addy, you haven't been feeling well since we left Africa. Maybe you picked up some strange virus. Or maybe a bug?"

"No," she answered, trying not to smile at the look on his face. "What I have is quite common. The doctor says I should be fine in about seven months."

"Seven months," Mac bellowed. "What kind of crackpot doctor did you go to?"

"An obstetrician," she said quietly, waiting for the words to sink in. Mac looked at her long and hard for a moment. He swallowed nervously a few times.

"An ob-ob..." He couldn't get the word out.

"Obstetrician," she repeated, trying to help him.

"You mean I'm—we're—we're pregnant?" His face broke into a wide smile as Addy nodded her head. "Oh, Addy!" He scooped her from the chair and twirled her around.

"Mac," she cautioned, and he came to an immediate halt. If the thought of flying made her green, getting spun in circles until she was dizzy and nearly breathless was about to make her turn purple.

"Oh, my goodness." Mac gently set her down on the chair. "Did I hurt you?" He asked hurriedly, his eyes going over her as if she were a piece of china.

"No," Addy assured him. "I'm fine, Mac. Really. I've just got a case of good old-fashioned morning sickness."

"But it's afternoon," Mac protested, glancing at his watch to be sure.

Addy laughed. "No matter what time it is, Mac, it's the same thing."

"A baby," he said softly, his eyes shining with love. "Why didn't you tell me?"

She looked at him quizzically. "Honey, I just did. I only found out this morning. And then when I went to see Grandpa, and discovered him missing, I was so upset, it completely slipped my mind."

"A baby," Mac said again, shaking his head in awe. "This is wonderful, Addy." He looked at her in confusion. "But how, I mean, when—"

Addy stood up and wrapped her arms around her husband. "Tonight, when you come home I'll show you...how." She lifted her mouth for his kiss, moving closer to him and marveling at how much her love for him grew every day. She couldn't imagine ever being happier. And now, with a baby on the way— A sudden thought jarred her. "Oh, Mac, there's just one more thing."

He frowned, not liking the mischievous look in her eyes. "What?"

"It seems Aunt Myrtle and Walter have a little favor to ask you."

Mac looked at her suspiciously. "What kind of a favor?"

Addy tried to keep a smile off her face. "Well, they were wondering if you would consider letting them help us name the baby."

Mac was thoughtful for a moment. "I don't think there would be any harm in that." He looked at her carefully. "Wait a minute, why do I have a feeling I've just been bushwhacked?"

Addy laughed and hooked her arm through his as she walked toward the door. "Well, you see, Aunt Myrtle confided that Walter's kind of partial to the name Nat."

"Nat." Mac frowned. Coming from a woman who named a pigeon Walter, he had expected something a bit more bizarre. "Nat's not so bad," he said slowly, not sure he wasn't being bushwhacked again.

Addy tried to arrange her face in a serious posture. "And for a middle name, Walter thought King might be nice."

Mac came to an abrupt halt. "What kind of middle name is King? Wait a minute." He was just putting two and two together. "Are you trying to tell me—Aunt Myrtle wants us to name our baby *Nat King Cole*!"

Addy chuckled. "He was her absolute all-time favorite singer," she explained hurriedly, trying not to laugh at his expression. "Well, I must admit, it was better than her first choice."

One dark eyebrow shot up. Mac couldn't wait to hear this one. "And what was her first choice?"

"Ice."

"Ice?" Mac laughed. "As in Ice Cole?"

"Then of course, there was her third choice," Addy went on, but Mac wasn't listening. He was drawing her into the circle of his arms.

"I love you, Addy."

"I love you, too, Mac," she whispered, placing his hand on her stomach. "We both love you."

*   *   *   *   *

COMING NEXT MONTH

#694 ETHAN—Diana Palmer—A Diamond Jubilee Title!
Don't miss *Ethan*—he's one Long, Tall Texan who'll have your heart roped and tied!

#695 GIVEAWAY GIRL—Val Whisenand
Private investigator Mike Dixon never meant to fall in love with Amy Alexander. How could he possibly tell her the painful truth about her mysterious past?

#696 JAKE'S CHILD—Lindsay Longford
The moment Jake Donnelly arrived with a bedraggled child, Sarah Jane Simpson felt a strange sense of foreboding. Could the little boy be her long-lost son?

#697 DEARLY BELOVED—Jane Bierce
Rebecca Hobbs thought a visit to her sleepy southern hometown would be restful. But handsome minister Frank Andrews had her heart working overtime!

#698 HONEYMOON HIDEAWAY—Linda Varner
Divorce lawyer Sam Knight was convinced that true love was a myth. But Libby Turner, a honeymoon hideaway manager, was set to prove him wrong with one kiss as evidence....

#699 NO HORSING AROUND—Stella Bagwell
Jacqui Prescott was determined to show cynical Spencer Matlock she was a capable jockey. But then she found herself suddenly longing to come in first in the sexy trainer's heart!

AVAILABLE THIS MONTH:

#688 FATHER CHRISTMAS
Mary Blayney

#689 DREAM AGAIN OF LOVE
Phyllis Halldorson

#690 MAKE ROOM FOR NANNY
Carol Grace

#691 MAKESHIFT MARRIAGE
Janet Franklin

#692 TEN DAYS IN PARADISE
Karen Leabo

#693 SWEET ADELINE
Sharon De Vita

Silhouette Romances®

DIAMOND JUBILEE
CELEBRATION!

It's Silhouette Books' tenth anniversary, and what better way to celebrate than to toast *you*, our readers, for making it all possible. Each month in 1990, we'll present you with a DIAMOND JUBILEE Silhouette Romance written by an all-time favorite author!

Welcome the new year with *Ethan*—a LONG, TALL TEXANS book by Diana Palmer. February brings Brittany Young's *The Ambassador's Daughter*. Look for *Never on Sundae* by Rita Rainville in March, and in April you'll find *Harvey's Missing* by Peggy Webb. Victoria Glenn, Lucy Gordon, Annette Broadrick, Dixie Browning and many more have special gifts of love waiting for you with their DIAMOND JUBILEE Romances.

Be sure to look for the distinctive DIAMOND JUBILEE emblem, and share in Silhouette's celebration. Saying thanks has never been so romantic....

Diana Palmer brings you an Award of Excellence title... and the first Silhouette Romance DIAMOND JUBILEE book.

ETHAN
by Diana Palmer

This month, Diana Palmer continues her bestselling LONG, TALL TEXANS series with *Ethan*—the story of a rugged rancher who refuses to get roped and tied by Arabella Craig, the one woman he can't resist.

The Award of Excellence is given to one specially selected title per month. Spend January with *Ethan* #694... a special DIAMOND JUBILEE title... only in Silhouette Romance.

Ethan-1

You'll flip . . . your pages won't!
Read paperbacks *hands-free* with

Book Mate • I

The perfect "mate" for all your romance paperbacks

Traveling • Vacationing • At Work • In Bed • Studying • Cooking • Eating

Perfect size for all standard paperbacks, this wonderful invention makes reading a pure pleasure! Ingenious design holds paperback books OPEN and FLAT so even wind can't ruffle pages – leaves your hands free to do other things. Reinforced, wipe-clean vinyl-covered holder flexes to let you turn pages without undoing the strap... supports paperbacks so well, they have the strength of hardcovers!

Pages turn WITHOUT opening the strap

SEE-THROUGH STRAP

Reinforced back stays flat

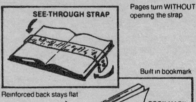

Built in bookmark

BOOK MARK

BACK COVER HOLDING STRIP

10" x 7¼" opened.
Snaps closed for easy carrying. too

SILHOUETTE DESIRE™
presents
AUNT EUGENIA'S TREASURES
by CELESTE HAMILTON

Liz, Cassandra and Maggie are the honored recipients of Aunt Eugenia's heirloom jewels...but Eugenia knows the real prizes are the young women themselves. Read about Aunt Eugenia's quest to find them everlasting love. Each book shines on its own, but together, they're priceless!

Available in December:
THE DIAMOND'S SPARKLE (SD #537)

Altruistic Liz Patterson wants nothing to do with Nathan Hollister, but as the fast-lane PR man tells Liz, love is something he's willing to take *very* slowly.

Available in February:
RUBY FIRE (SD #549)

Impulsive Cassandra Martin returns from her travels... ready to rekindle the flame with the man she never forgot, Daniel O'Grady.

Available in April:
THE HIDDEN PEARL (SD #561)

Cautious Maggie O'Grady comes out of her shell...and glows in the precious warmth of love when brazen Jonah Pendleton moves in next door.

Wonderful, luxurious gifts can be yours with proofs-of-purchase from any specially marked "Indulge A Little" Harlequin or Silhouette book with the Offer Certificate properly completed, plus a check or money order (do not send cash) to cover postage and handling payable to Harlequin/Silhouette "Indulge A Little, Give A Lot" Offer. We will send you the specified gift.

Mail-in-Offer

OFFER CERTIFICATE

Item	A Collector's Doll	B Soaps in a Basket	C Potpourri Sachet	D Scented Hangers
# of Proofs-of-Purchase	18	12	6	4
Postage & Handling	$3.25	$2.75	$2.25	$2.00
Check One				

Name _____

Address _____ Apt # _____

City _____ State _____ Zip _____

ONE PROOF OF PURCHASE

To collect your free gift by mail you must include the necessary number of proofs-of-purchase plus postage and handling with offer certificate

SR-3

Harlequin®/Silhouette®

Mail this certificate, designated number of proofs-of-purchase and check or money order for postage and handling to:

INDULGE A LITTLE
P.O. Box 9055
Buffalo, N.Y. 14269-9055